Amy, Number Seven

MARILYN KAYE

BANTAM BOOKS
NEW YORK • TORONTO • LONDON • SYDNEY • AUCKLAND

RL 5.5, 008–012
AMY, NUMBER SEVEN
A Bantam Skylark Book / November 1998

ISBN 0-553-49238-1

Published simultaneously in the United States and Canada.

Bantam Books are published by Bantam Books, a division of Bantam Doubleday Dell Publishing Group, Inc. Its trademark, consisting of the words "Bantam Books" and the portrayal of a rooster, is Registered in U.S. Patent and Trademark Office and in other countries. Marca Registrada. Bantam Books, 1540 Broadway, New York, New York 10036.

PRINTED IN THE UNITED STATES OF AMERICA

OPM   0   9   8   7   6   5   4   3   2   1

*Dedicated with affection and gratitude to The Group:
Anne Adams Lang, Jane Furse, Bette Glenn, Katherine
Leiner, JoAnne McFarland, Lavinia Plonka, Gretta
Keene Sabinson, and Michele Willens*

Amy, Number Seven

prologue

The director was handed a file. He opened it, examined the few pages inside, and then closed it. "Why are you showing me this? The project was terminated twelve years ago."

"It may be reopened."

"Why? All material was destroyed in the fire."

"There is evidence that something may have survived."

The director looked up with interest. "Something? Or someone?"

"That is what we want you to find out."

 one

Amy didn't know how she had arrived at this place. She didn't know where she was, or why she was there. But she knew she had been there before, many, many times, so she wasn't frightened.

She lay flat on her back. She could hear the faint, familiar, rhythmic sounds, like a muffled drumbeat, and she could see white all around. She couldn't discern distinct objects, though. The glass blurred her vision.

She was surrounded by glass, thick glass. If she thrust out an arm, or kicked up a leg, she could almost touch it.

It didn't bother her, being inside glass. She knew the glass protected her, although she wasn't quite sure what she needed protection from. Where she lay was soft, warm, and comfortable. The air was sweet to breathe, her stomach was full, she was safe and secure.

But no. Something was happening, something that had never happened before. A streak of red-orange color had slashed through the whiteness. Then there were more streaks. She heard a new sound, a crackling sound. And now she was getting warmer, too warm.

Fire! There was a fire blowing beyond the glass. It was getting bigger, it was moving closer. She tried to cry out, but she had no voice. She tried to move, but her body wouldn't obey her brain. Somehow she knew the fire would be stronger than the glass, that the glass wouldn't protect her anymore. She was trapped. She would be consumed by the flames. She would cease to exist. She experienced a new feeling, fear; and she began to shake.

Maybe it was the shaking that woke her. With an effort, she forced herself to sit upright. She was still trembling, and despite the light breeze that came through her open bedroom window, she was sweating.

But there was no glass, no fire. From the faint glow of a streetlight that filtered through her curtains, she could make out her shadow in the mirror that hung on her closet door. There was her desk, and her bookcase, and her old collection of Barbies. In the confusion of her mind, the one clear thought was that she really should get rid of them. At the age of twelve, she no longer played with Barbies.

She switched on the lamp, climbed out of bed, and on shaky legs made her way to the mirror. The reflection was reassuring. She was a little pale, and beads of sweat had accumulated on her forehead, but she was still Amy Candler. Five feet tall, a hundred pounds. Two eyes, brown; two ears, one nose, one mouth, straight teeth; straight hair, also brown. She was completely normal and ordinary in every way—except for the fact that she kept having the same dream again and again, at least once a month, sometimes more. The whiteness, the glass, the soft drums—she was accustomed to that. But this time something new had been added—the fire.

She was calmer now, but all that sweating and trembling had left her very thirsty.

Water from the sink in the bathroom wouldn't do— she wanted the cold, fizzy kind that was in the refrigerator. She tiptoed down the hall, holding her breath as she neared her mother's bedroom. Nancy Candler had a sixth sense about her daughter—she always seemed to know when Amy got up at night.

Amy went down the stairs, through the living room, and then through the dining room. In the kitchen she switched on a bright overhead light, went to the refrigerator, and took out the bottled water. She poured some in a glass and drank it thirstily. Then she poured some more.

Next to her own room, the kitchen was her favorite

place in the house. She liked the wallpaper, with its pattern of sunflowers and daisies, and the yellow-and-white checked curtains. Pots and pans hung from hooks in the ceiling, and in the center was an old-fashioned carved wooden table with four chairs. In the kitchen, Amy could pretend that she lived in a country cottage in the woods, not in half of a duplex in a West Los Angeles condominium community.

Her mother had put a lot of work into this kitchen. On one wall were wooden shelves she'd found at an antique fair, and on the shelves were photographs in antique frames. With the glass of water still in her hand, Amy went across the room to look at the pictures.

She'd seen them a zillion times, but they always made her feel good, sort of cozy. They were mostly photos of her, at every age, sometimes alone, sometimes with her mother. There was a photo of her mother alone—her graduation picture from the university.

There was only one photo of her father. He looked so young—probably because he *was* young, only twenty-three when the picture was taken. He was very handsome in his military uniform. For the umpteenth time, Amy wished she could have inherited his curly blond hair.

She wondered what he would look like now. She could never know. He'd died, less than a year after this photo was taken, just two months before she was born.

He didn't die in a war—there weren't any wars going on when he was in the army. It was a dumb car accident, her mother told her. If he'd died in a battle, they would have had medals and certificates to remember him by. But because he'd died in a regular accident in some little country far away, they had nothing, not even a grave to visit. There were no other photos of him either, not even a wedding photo of her parents. Her mother said there had been a fire in the attic of the house where they lived, before Amy was born, and every picture, every memento of Steven Candler had been consumed in the blaze. Maybe that was why fire had come into Amy's dream this time, turning her dream into a nightmare.

The photo she was looking at now, the only one they had, didn't tell Amy much about her father. It was a formal, posed picture, like the photos taken for the school yearbook, where everyone looked fake. Their smiles weren't sincere. She searched his face for something, anything that might reveal his character, but it was hopeless. She couldn't see anything of herself in him either. She wished she could make some sort of connection to him. But as hard as she would stare at the photo, he remained just a nice-looking man, a stranger.

When she was younger, she used to ask her mother questions about him, but she never got very satisfying answers. Was he nice? Yes. Did he tell jokes? Sometimes. Could he turn cartwheels? I don't remember. What was his favorite flavor of ice cream? Strawberry, her mother had told her. But then, another time, when she asked the same question, her mother had said chocolate chip. It bothered Amy that her mother's memory was so unclear.

She put the photo back on the shelf and moved on to the window. Was there a full moon tonight? she wondered. Her best friend and neighbor, Tasha Morgan, once told Amy that there were legends about full moons, that weird things could happen then. People could turn into werewolves, or have visions, or just go crazy. A long time ago, when Amy told Tasha about her dream, Tasha had suggested that maybe the full moon was responsible. Amy had never checked to see if the moon was full on the nights when she had the dreams. She never took Tasha's stories very seriously—her friend had a wild imagination. But she decided to check on the phase of the moon anyway.

She drew back the checked curtain, but before she could begin searching the sky, something else caught her eye.

There was a man on the sidewalk across the street, facing her house. He was looking through a camera, and the camera was aimed directly at her. Then a light flashed.

Amy dropped the glass of water and cried out. She let go of the curtain so it would cover the window again.

"Amy? Amy, is that you?" The frantic voice came from the stairs. A second later, Nancy Candler was in the kitchen. "Amy, what's wrong?"

"I saw someone."

"You saw someone? Where?" Her mother looked around the room wildly.

Amy pointed a trembling finger at the window. "Out there." She looked away as Nancy pulled the curtain back.

"I don't see anyone."

"The man with the camera."

"Where?"

Was her mother blind? "Across the street!"

"Amy, it's pitch black out and there's no streetlight. Even if someone was standing there, you wouldn't be able to see him."

"But he was there! I did see him!" Now that she joined her mother at the window, Amy realized she was right. There was no way Amy could have seen anyone. She couldn't even make out the huge palm tree that she knew stood directly in front of their house.

But the flash from the camera . . . it had happened, she was sure of that. Then she wasn't so sure. A firefly could have made that spark of light. And she could have fantasized the rest.

She was aware of her mother hovering over her. "What are you doing up at this hour?" her mother asked. She placed a hand on Amy's forehead. "Are you feeling all right?" Amy didn't know what her mother expected to learn from her forehead. As far as she could remember, she had never had a fever in her life.

"I'm okay."

But now her mother's voice became even more anxious. "Did you have that dream again?"

Amy had told Nancy once about the dream, and she'd regretted it ever since. Nancy had interrogated her about it, asking for all the details Amy could remember—was the glass warm or cool to the touch? Did she know what the drums meant? Did she recognize any other people in the dream? And now, anytime Amy woke up in a bad mood, Nancy would ask her if she'd had the dream again.

Amy didn't feel like answering questions now. "No, I just woke up and I was thirsty." It was then that she remembered the glass of water she'd dropped. She looked down and saw the shards of glass on the floor. Nancy saw them too and immediately went into action. "Don't move, your feet are bare." She pulled over a chair and instructed Amy to sit down with her feet up. Then she scurried about, picking up the larger pieces of glass gingerly and using a hand-held vacuum to clean up the rest.

Finally Amy was allowed to rise from her chair and go

back to bed. But she paused by the collection of photos. "Mom . . ."

Nancy was emptying the vacuum's contents into the wastebasket. "What?"

"Why don't you ever tell me about my father?"

There was a brief silence before Nancy responded. "What do you want to know?"

"Nothing in particular. I just wonder why you don't talk about him."

"Because . . . because I don't like to look back, Amy. I don't want to dwell on the past, and neither should you. What's done is done; it's over, finished. Why should we torture ourselves with our memories?"

"But I don't even have any memories!" Amy declared.

"So much the better," Nancy said. "You can look ahead to the future."

Moments later, lying in bed, Amy considered her mother's attitude. She could understand and appreciate Nancy's desire to move forward, not backward. But it still didn't explain her silence about her late husband. Most people liked remembering happy times in the past, even as they enjoyed life in the present and looked forward to more good times.

Of course, it was possible that her parents' marriage hadn't been such a happy one. When she thought about how many of her classmates came from divorced homes, she realized how unpleasant some marriages could be. Maybe Steven Candler hadn't been so nice. Or maybe he and Nancy just didn't get along very well.

But even if it had been a crummy marriage, even if Steven Candler had been a creep, he was still her father and she wanted to know more about him. Was her mother ever planning to tell her anything?

Drowsiness was beginning to overcome her, and she didn't fight it. Maybe she'd dream about her father tonight.

But she fell asleep and dreamed about nothing at all.

two 2

The doorbell rang the next morning at precisely 8:07, according to Amy's digital watch. Amy leaped up from her chair at the breakfast table. "There's Tasha, I gotta go."

But Nancy hadn't finished the questions she'd been asking since Amy got up that morning. She followed Amy to the door.

"The man you saw last night," she began again, and then she amended that to, "the man you *thought* you saw last night. Did you recognize him? Had you ever seen him before?"

Amy picked up her backpack and slung it over her shoulder. "Mom, how could I recognize him if I didn't really see him? It was just my imagination. You said so yourself, remember?"

"Well, maybe you saw him in your dreams."

Amy opened the door while her mother was speaking, and Tasha caught those last words. "Did you see someone in a dream?" she asked eagerly. Tasha had recently read a book about dream interpretation, and she was very enthusiastic about the subject.

"You're late," Amy told her sternly.

"Two minutes," Tasha said. "Don't worry, it's not going to affect your perfect attendance record."

Nancy was examining the sky. "Do you have an umbrella, Amy? I think I see clouds."

But Amy had already started down the walkway, and she ignored the question. "Bye, Mom!" She didn't allow herself a sigh of relief until she glanced back and saw that her mother had gone inside.

"What do you think of my cap?" Tasha asked her.

Baseball-style caps were very big at Parkside Middle School that year. The odder they were, the better. Tasha's new cap was denim blue and read Oscar's Auto Parts. Amy was wearing an ordinary L.A. Dodgers cap, and just about everyone had one of those.

"Cool," Amy replied. They were turning the corner now, and a woman Amy had never seen before came out of a condo to pick up the newspaper on her step. She waved at them, and Tasha waved back.

"Who's that?" Amy asked.

"She moved in on Saturday," Tasha told her. "Her name's Monica Jackson, and she's an artist."

"She looks like an artist," Amy said, turning to get another glimpse of the woman. Her hair was a kind of red that no one had ever been born with, and it stuck out in all directions. She was wearing some kind of shirt and pants printed with leopard spots—Amy wasn't sure if they were pajamas or real clothes. "How do you know her?"

"I saw the moving van, so I came over and introduced myself. She's very cool, and she showed me some of her paintings. They're weird. She makes jewelry too."

"Is the jewelry weird?"

"I don't know, I didn't see any of it. Maybe we can go over there after school and she'll show us some stuff. She said I could come by anytime, and bring friends."

Amy marveled at the way Tasha could meet people so easily. Amy didn't think she could ever go up to a complete stranger and start talking like Tasha did. It wasn't that she was shy; she had no problem speaking up in class or meeting other kids. It was just . . . well, she really didn't know why she had these funny feelings about adult strangers.

"What kind of dream did you have last night?" Tasha asked her.

"Oh, it was nothing," Amy said, momentarily forgetting that she'd once told Tasha about her recurring dreams.

"Was it the old one, when you're in a glass cage?"

"Yeah. It's not a cage, exactly. I don't know what it is."

"I haven't been able to find out what that means," Tasha told her. "There's nothing about glass in my book. I heard about a Web site for dream interpretation, and I'm going to check it out."

"Something new happened last night," Amy said. "There was a fire, outside the glass. That was never part of the dream before."

"A fire!" Tasha pondered that. "Interesting. I'll bet it's got something to do with puberty."

"You think everything has something to do with puberty," Amy pointed out.

"Well, it's a pretty big deal," Tasha said. "Your body's changing, your hormones are going crazy, emotionally you're a total wreck. Did you hear about Kelly Brankowski in geography in Friday? She started crying, just because she didn't know the main exports of Peru. That's what happens when you're going through puberty."

Sometimes Amy wished Tasha didn't read quite so much. "Yeah, okay." There was something else she wanted to discuss. "Listen, Tasha . . . has your mother been acting weird lately?"

"Weirder than usual?"

"Not weird exactly, more like nervous. My mother keeps looking at me like . . . like she's scared of what she's going to see. As if I'm about to explode or turn green or something."

Tasha nodded understandingly. "Yeah, my mother looks at me like that too. It's puberty."

"Tasha! You can't blame everything on puberty!"

"Practically everything," Tasha insisted. "Your mother and my mother know what's happening, or what's about to happen. They're watching for the signs. You know, like bad moods and acne. Hair. Breasts." She lowered her voice. "Menstruation."

Tasha could be right, Amy thought. It could be difficult for mothers to see their daughters changing so much. "But all that stuff is natural. And my mother teaches biology, for crying out loud. She knows all about bodies changing. Why would she act so nervous about it?"

Tasha had no answer for that. "Sarah Klein got her period last week," she reported. "I told my mother, and you know what she said? She didn't get hers until she was fourteen, which means I could be really late too. I don't know if I think that's good or bad. I mean, when you get your period, you know you're a real woman, and that's good. But it sounds kind of messy."

"My mother said I could get mine any day now," Amy said.

"Did she get her period when she was twelve?"

"I guess. How else would she know?"

"Well, she *is* a biologist. Like you said, she must know a lot about human bodies. I wonder if Jeanine Bryant has her period yet."

Amy considered this. Jeanine was certainly looking more mature lately. Just last Friday, she'd showed up in homeroom with turquoise eye shadow extending from her lashes to her brows. Of course, that had nothing to do with her body changing. And anyway, their teacher had made her go to the rest room and wash it off.

"If Jeanine got her period, everyone would know about it," Amy decided. Jeanine was notorious for bragging about herself. "Besides, she's not even twelve yet."

"But she will be, very soon," Tasha pointed out. "Did you get an invitation to her birthday party?"

Amy nodded. "Why is she having it at an ice-skating rink?"

"Because she's been taking ice-skating lessons," Tasha told her.

"Well, that's good for *her*," Amy said. "But what about the rest of us? I've never ice-skated before."

"I haven't either," Tasha declared. "In fact, I can't think of anyone who knows how to ice-skate. I mean, it's not exactly something you grow up doing in southern California. I can't figure out why she invited me anyway. It's not like we're friends."

Amy agreed. "Neither can I. She practically *hates* me."

Tasha didn't argue with that. Everyone knew there was a competition between Amy and Jeanine, and it had been going on since first grade. They had been rivals for prizes at school, for class elections and roles in the school plays, in gymnastics, and lately, for attention from boys.

"Actually, I think I do know why we were invited," Tasha said. "She wants to show off how well she can skate now, so we'll all stand around and go 'ooh' and 'ahh.' You know she'll be happy if you fall on your butt while she spins around like Tara Lipinski."

"You're probably right," Amy admitted. "I'm not saying she's going to skate like Tara Lipinski. But I'll fall on my butt."

"I doubt that," Tasha said. "You're always good in sports."

"Not when I don't know what I'm doing," Amy told her. "There's a big difference between ice-skating and playing volleyball."

"I can think of another reason why she invited us," Tasha commented. "Her mother probably made her invite all the girls in our class."

That made sense to Amy. Mrs. Bryant was very social, and she was a big shot in the community. She wouldn't risk offending parents by not inviting their daughters to the party.

Then Amy frowned.

"What's the matter?" Tasha asked.

"Don't you hear that?"

"Hear what?"

She couldn't say exactly. A pounding, like someone running. Running behind them, coming toward them, getting closer . . .

A second later, Tasha's fourteen-year-old brother, Eric, was beside them. "Race you to school," he suggested.

"Make like the wind and blow," Tasha replied.

He did, but not before snatching the cap off Tasha's head. Tasha shrieked and started running after him. Amy joined the pursuit.

It was good to run. She pulled off her own cap so it wouldn't fall, and her long hair lifted off her shoulders and felt less heavy. For the first time, she noticed how the houses and gardens and cars flew past and created a blur of colors. She'd left Tasha behind, but that wasn't unusual. Tasha's legs were shorter and she wasn't much of an athlete.

What did surprise her was how close she was getting to Eric. Eric was two years older, at least five inches taller, and he was a boy—and she was actually getting close to catching up with him!

Eric looked over his shoulder. His eyes widened when

he saw that Amy was near. He was so surprised that he stopped altogether.

"Hey, you can run!"

Amy stopped, too, and felt her face growing warm. She'd known Eric forever, and he'd never paid her a compliment before. She didn't know what to say. If she said thank you, he might turn the compliment into a joke, maybe even an insult.

She treated the comment carelessly. "Yeah, whatever."

"No, I mean, you can *really* run. Most girls your age can't run that fast."

She decided to ignore the patronizing way he said "girls your age." "So what?"

"So maybe you should go out for track."

"Track?"

"Running, stupid. In competition. I'm on the boys' track team at Parkside."

"Is there a girls' track team?"

"No, but maybe you could start one."

Amy was flattered, but she didn't take his idea too seriously. Gymnastics was her sport, and she didn't even give that enough practice time. Coach Persky was always yelling at her for not working at it hard enough.

Tasha finally reached them. She was huffing and puffing, and she was furious. "Give me my cap!" she shrieked at Eric.

Eric tossed it to her, but he kept his eyes on Amy.

"We've got track practice after school today. You should come by and talk to our coach."

"We've got gymnastics after school today," Tasha reminded her.

"Yeah," Amy said. "Sorry, Eric." She really was sorry too. She wouldn't mind hanging out a little with Eric. It was funny—just a year ago, she never thought of him as anyone except Tasha's annoying brother.

They all proceeded to school peacefully. By the time they reached the teachers' parking lot, they'd joined the general mob of seventh-, eighth-, and ninth-graders moving toward the open doors at the main entrance of the modern, sprawling one-story building. The noise level was particularly high, since this was a Monday and kids were greeting each other with more enthusiasm than usual. Like Tasha and Eric, Amy looked around the crowd, and she waved and yelled to special friends.

She stopped walking so abruptly that two girls walking just behind bumped into her.

"Sorry," they chorused, but Amy didn't respond. She recognized someone, and it wasn't a special friend.

A man stood by the wide steps leading to the entrance doors. He was peering through the lens of a camera, and he seemed to be taking random shots of kids walking into school. Some students didn't see him, others ignored him, and some paused and posed with a smile or their tongues sticking out.

More people were bumping into Amy as she remained frozen in place. "Amy, are you okay?" Tasha asked.

"That man . . ."

"What man?"

Was she seeing things again? "The man by the steps, taking pictures!"

"Oh, yeah. What about him?"

At least she wasn't imagining this time. "I've seen him before."

"Where?" Eric asked.

She hesitated. "I *thought* I saw him. In the middle of the night, across the street from my house, taking pictures. But when I looked a second time, no one was there, and my mother said I was just half-asleep."

"Wait a minute," Eric said. "You *thought* you saw this guy, then you think you didn't, and now you think you see him again?"

She realized how silly she must sound. "Well, yeah. Sort of."

"How can you recognize him?" Tasha asked. "Even with my glasses on, I can't see his face from here."

Tasha was right. The man was practically hidden in the shadow of the canopy that hung over the school entrance. There was no way Amy could have gotten a good look at him.

She felt unbelievably stupid, and not just because she

was imagining things again. She continued to walk with Tasha and Eric. "What is he doing?" she asked.

"Taking pictures," Tasha said.

"I *know* that. Why is he taking pictures?"

"Maybe he's the photographer for the yearbook. Or maybe he's from a newspaper, or a magazine that's doing an article on middle-school style!" Tasha patted her curls. "How do I look?"

Amy didn't answer. They were about to climb the steps now—and come directly into the range of the camera. Instinctively she averted her face, turning away from the man so he couldn't possibly photograph her.

"What did you do that for?" Tasha asked as they entered the school.

Amy replied with the first thought that came to her mind. "He gave me the creeps."

Eric gave her an odd look. "You're nuts," he said succinctly, and moved on to join some friends.

Amy looked at Tasha. "He's probably right. I don't know why I'm so jumpy."

"You're not nuts," Tasha said comfortingly. "It's just puberty."

t͟h͟ree
3

Middle school was a lot better than elementary school, in Amy's opinion. She particularly liked the fact that they weren't stuck in one room with one teacher all day. From 8:20 to 8:35, there was homeroom. Ms. Weller took attendance, handed out official school stuff, and made them quiet down when announcements from the office came over the intercom. They got ten minutes to change rooms between periods, which was just enough time to stop at the water fountain or the rest room, exchange a little news with a friend in the hall, and brush hair.

From 8:45 to 9:35 was math, one of Amy's favorite classes. Math had always come easily to her, and she could never understand why other kids had problems understanding it. She always seemed to know the answers before anyone else did, but she'd learned to keep her mouth shut—no one liked a show-off.

At 9:45, she had geography, one of her least favorite classes, but not because it was difficult at all. The teacher was just boring. He read to them from the text-book, and Amy had discovered that if she read a chapter ahead of time, she knew exactly what he would say.

After geography was English, with Ms. Weller again. This was a class that required more effort from her. In math and geography, she dealt with facts that were either right or wrong. In English, she had to write essays, with opinions and ideas and interpretations. Ms. Weller was big on creativity and originality. She praised Amy's perfect punctuation and spelling, but she was constantly telling Amy to "respond" to the literature she read.

Their last assignment had been a biographical essay. Ms. Weller had told the students to pick someone notable. But they couldn't just describe why the person was famous—they had to write about why they believed this person was remarkable and worthy of remembering, and they had to announce in class who their subjects were. Amy recalled how Jeanine sneered when she said she'd be writing about Helen Keller. Three other girls had already declared their intentions of writing about Helen Keller, so Amy knew Helen Keller was a pretty safe topic—mainly because it was easy to point out why she was deserving of honor. She was practically a saint. Of course, Jeanine topped that—*she* was going to write about Mother Teresa.

While Amy was writing the essay, she realized, for the first time, what Ms. Weller expected, what she meant by originality, creativity, and interpretation. This experience provided her with revelations, and as a result, the essay had a whole different sound to it. She would be getting it back today and was anxious to see if she was now on the right track.

Apparently she was. The essays were returned just after the bell rang, and the cover sheet displayed not only a big red A, but also a comment: "Excellent, very interesting observations, a tremendous improvement!"

Jeanine Bryant was sitting right next to Amy. Amy slipped her paper across to the edge of the desk so Jeanine could get a clear view of her A. Maybe it wasn't nice to be a show-off, but with Jeanine, she figured it was okay. Jeanine was the biggest show-off in the universe.

Sure enough, when Amy looked she saw that Jeanine had already positioned *her* paper so that Amy could see that she got an A too. The two girls looked at each other and exchanged fake smiles of congratulation. Amy was sure they were both thinking the same thing—that someday, Ms. Weller would give one of them an A+, and then they'd really know who was best.

The class discussion that day was all about biographies. Toward the end of the period, Ms. Weller asked, "Who can tell me the difference between a biography and an autobiography?"

Jeanine's hand went up before Amy's could.

"Yes, Jeanine?"

"A biography is the history of a life told by another person. An autobiography is when a person writes about his own life."

"His or *her* life," Ms. Weller corrected. Amy couldn't resist a little smirk. "But you are correct, Jeanine." Now Jeanine could toss Amy a look of triumph.

"For your next assignment," Ms. Weller continued, "I want each of you to write an autobiography."

Dwayne Hicks, who sat in the back of the room and was extremely cute, raised his hand. "Who are we supposed to write about?"

Amy grimaced at the kids who giggled. Dwayne might not be a mental giant, but he looked like Leonardo DiCaprio and therefore deserved some respect.

Ms. Weller was patient. "What did Jeanine just tell us, Dwayne? When a person writes about his or her own life, this is an autobiography. So when I tell you to write an autobiography, this means I want you to write about . . . who?"

"Me?" Dwayne asked.

"Exactly."

Class clown Alan Greenfield yelled out, "You mean, we all have to write essays about Dwayne?"

Everyone laughed, and Ms. Weller managed a long-suffering smile. "Very funny, Alan. Now, I want these essays to be at least ten pages . . ." In anticipation, she held up her hand to ward off the groans. "But you will have two weeks, not one, to complete this assignment. And each of you will present an oral summary of your written autobiography in class." This announcement was greeted with another groan, a little louder and more heartfelt.

Amy raised her hand. "Exactly what do we have to write about ourselves?"

"It's impossible to say 'exactly,' " Ms. Weller told her. "There are no rules to writing an autobiography. Generally a person writes about the history of their family, their ancestry. Some people go way back, to centuries before they were born. Then they move on to their birth, and growth, and the important events in their life. Since everyone's life is different, no two autobiographies are the same. Some writers might exaggerate some aspects of their lives, or omit the parts they don't feel are interesting. They might play up events that make them look good and play down events that make them look not so good. I want you to research yourselves as well as you can. Talk to parents, grandparents, aunts, and uncles. Learn about your early years, and how you developed."

"Developed?" a girl asked faintly, and a couple of boys uttered nasty laughs.

Ms. Weller frowned. "I'm talking about your growth, walking, talking. What were your first words, that sort of thing. Write about your hobbies, your special interests, your talents. Write about what you hope to accomplish, how you intend to work toward your goals, how you hope to achieve them."

Amy glanced at Jeanine. She was smiling serenely, nodding, looking like she'd already written the autobiography in her head. Amy couldn't look quite so confident.

The bell rang, signaling the end of class. As she got up from her desk, Amy heard the teacher call out to her. "Could I see you a moment, Amy?"

Amy went to the teacher's desk. Practically everyone had left the room by now, but Ms. Weller still kept her voice low. "Amy, I have something to ask you. About the essay I returned today . . ." She seemed uncomfortable, as if she was unsure how to say what she wanted to say.

"Was there something wrong with it, Ms. Weller?"

"No . . . in fact, it was just about perfect. Amy . . . was it your own work?"

"You mean, did I write it myself?"

Ms. Weller nodded.

"Of course I did!"

"You didn't copy any of it, from a book or an encyclopedia?"

Amy was speechless. At the beginning of the term, Ms. Weller had told them about plagiarism. She was horrified to think that Ms. Weller might be accusing her of that.

Ms. Weller must have seen the shock in her face, because she hastened to reassure her. "I'm sorry, Amy. I should have known you wouldn't do anything like that. It's just that, well, your essay was so outstanding, so very professional and mature . . ." she smiled. "I suppose I'll just have to accept the fact that I have a very talented student."

Amy smiled uncertainly, thanked the teacher, and left the room. That was strange, she thought. But she wasn't sure what was stranger—being accused of plagiarism or discovering she had a talent for writing. And it happened so fast! She hadn't even been trying that hard to improve!

But she couldn't spend any time congratulating herself. In two weeks, when they turned in their autobiographies, Ms. Weller could be changing her opinion dramatically. Amy was glad she had her lunch period next, so she could share her trepidations with Tasha.

"I don't see why you're so worried," Tasha declared after Amy told her about the next assignment. "It's your own life, you don't have to make anything up. Just write down everything that's happened to you."

"But that's just it," Amy said. "There isn't anything to write down. Nothing's ever happened to me. Nothing interesting, at least. What am I going to write about? Going to the beach last summer? Everyone does that!"

"Gymnastics?" Tasha suggested.

"Practically everyone does that too. And it's not like I'm in training for the Olympics."

"Write about your family."

"What family? My mother teaches biology, big deal. I don't have any brothers or sisters. I don't even have any aunts or uncles or cousins."

"Grandparents?"

Amy shook her head.

"Dead?"

"I guess so," Amy said. "My mother was an orphan. And I guess I'd know if my father's parents were alive." She frowned. "I don't even know their names. We don't have any photos. They all burned up in a fire before I was born."

"You could write about your father," Tasha said. "He died young. That's sort of interesting."

"But I don't know anything about him. When I ask my mother, she practically freaks out."

"How sad," Tasha murmured. She removed her glasses,

and her brown eyes were moist. "She truly loved him, and she can't bear to talk about him. It's so tragic."

"Or maybe she hated his guts and can't stand remembering him," Amy pointed out. "In any case, I've got nothing to write about. Except for my mother, there's nobody who can tell me anything."

Tasha considered the situation. "How about your pediatrician?"

"My what?"

"Your pediatrician, your doctor. I've been going to Dr. Hanson since I was born; she knows everything about me."

"I don't have a pediatrician," Amy told her.

Tasha's eyes widened. "Amy! I can't believe you didn't tell me!"

"Tell you what?"

"You're going to a gynecologist already!"

"No, I'm not going to a gynecologist," Amy told her. "I don't have any kind of doctor."

"Who do you see when you're sick?"

"I'm never sick."

Tasha gazed at her curiously. "You know, I never realized that before, but you're right. You never got chicken pox and mumps like the rest of the kids in elementary school, did you?"

"No, I'm very healthy. I've never even had a cavity."

"Well, still, you must have been to a doctor some-time," Tasha said. "For a checkup, at least."

"I don't remember ever having a checkup," Amy replied.

"You *had* to have a checkup to start school when you were four or five," Tasha insisted. "It's the law. You had to have vaccinations and get tested for allergies and all that."

"I don't think so," Amy said doubtfully.

"I *know* so," Tasha stated firmly. "Remember last fall, when I had mono, and I had to stay out of phys ed for a month? Ms. Carroll, the assistant principal, made me stay in the office and staple things. Anyway, they've got these file drawers in there, and every student has a big fat folder. I saw the secretary and Ms. Carroll taking folders out and putting things in them all the time. Everything about you is in your folder. Like once, when I was in the office, Simone Cusack was sent home for doing something really terrible."

"Like what?" Amy asked with interest.

"I don't remember. She bit a substitute teacher or spit at her, or something like that. Anyway, I saw Ms. Carroll write a report about it and put it in Simone's folder. It will stay there forever and ever. Simone probably doesn't even know it's there."

"Did you ever look in your folder?"

"No. I wanted to, but it's, like, totally forbidden,

and someone was always in the office with me." She leaned forward. "Hey, there's an idea. Let's find out when the next faculty meeting is, and sneak into the office then. The secretary doesn't lock the door until she leaves for the day. I know which drawer the student folders are in. We'll get yours, look inside, and you'll find out something about yourself. At least your birth certificate will be in there. That gives your grandparents' names. And there's something in the file about who to notify in case of emergency. Whoever your mother put down must know something about you."

It was a tempting notion, but Amy shook her head. "What if we get caught? I've never broken a school rule in my entire life."

"Shhh," Tasha said suddenly, and spoke in a whisper. "Jeanine Bryant and Linda Riviera are coming."

For the next few seconds, the girls were silent, and both pretended to be fascinated by their Salisbury steaks. Jeanine, however, seemed to have no problem with the possibility of Amy overhearing her conversation.

"I think it'll be fun, creating an autobiography," Jeanine was saying loudly to Linda.

"Me too," Linda replied. "Do you have anything special you're going to write about?"

"Well, back when I was living in North Carolina, I was named Little Miss Princess of Tottom County when

I was five. And did you know that I've been taking harp lessons? My teacher says I have a lot of talent."

With that, the two girls moved on, leaving the cafeteria. Tasha looked at Amy meaningfully. "You'd better come up with *something*."

Like what? Amy wondered off and on for the rest of the day. She drifted from lunch to American history, to French, to art, and to phys ed, without coming up with any brilliant ideas. She supposed she could make up something about her life. Ms. Weller had said that some writers exaggerated. But she didn't think that meant she could down-and-out lie.

The assignment was still on her mind after school, when Tasha's mother picked them up and drove them to their gymnastics class. The class was held at a sports arena in Sunshine Square, a minimall twenty minutes from school. Among the class of fifteen girls, which met every Monday, Wednesday, and Friday afternoon, were five others from Parkside. Unfortunately, one of those girls was Jeanine.

"Don't say anything about my autobiography," Amy whispered to Tasha as they went into the arena. "I don't want Jeanine to know I'm having trouble."

"Are you kidding?" Tasha snorted. "At gymnastics, Jeanine doesn't want to talk about anything but gymnastics."

She was right. Jeanine's competitive streak was in full force here, even in the locker room, where the girls changed into their leotards. She prattled on and on, demonstrating her knowledge of the sport.

"Did you see that meet on TV Saturday, the one in Nevada? It was so amazing. Lucy Burroughs missed her dismount, and Gwen Daley lost her grip on the parallel bars. But Karina Jimenez scored nine point two on beam, so I think she's going to qualify for the next-level meet."

Amy had no idea who these people were, and she suspected no one else in the locker room did either. One girl, a couple of years older than them, looked at her scornfully as they moved out of the locker room and onto the floor. "There weren't any meets on TV Saturday."

Jeanine met her eyes with equal scorn. "Not on *regular* TV. But we have a satellite dish. We can get *everything*."

"Cut the chatter!" Coach Persky bellowed, and they were all immediately silent. The big, bearlike gymnastics coach was gruff, and he didn't spare anyone's feelings. They were all pretty much used to him, although occasionally a girl would burst into tears when his criticism was particularly harsh.

His criticisms were tough today, but not as biting as they could be. Even so, Amy prepared herself for a real attack when she began her approach to the vault. That was her toughest move, and she could never do it to Coach Persky's satisfaction. The fact that her sleep had been disrupted the night before, and that her thoughts were on that autobiography assignment, certainly couldn't improve her concentration.

So she was even more surprised than Coach Persky was when she executed a faultless approach, sailed over the vault, and landed lightly but firmly on the other side without the slightest tremble. She stood there frozen for a second, too startled to move.

"Do that again," Coach Persky ordered her.

It had to have been a fluke, she thought. She'd never be able to pull it off again.

But to her utter amazement, she did. She froze in her landing position, and like an electric shock, the thrill buzzed through her. This was incredible!

Clearly Coach Persky thought so too. He couldn't come up with any criticism at all.

"Well," he said roughly. "I see Candler's been practicing. Not bad, keep it up."

Coming from him, this was high praise. She didn't have to look to know that Jeanine's upper lip was curled in annoyance. Jeanine would do anything for a little attention from Coach Persky. It was all Amy could do to keep from jumping for joy.

Happily Tasha wasn't the jealous type. Standing in line for the balance beam, she whispered to Amy, "That was unbelievable! You were fantastic on the vault."

Amy didn't have to worry about acting like a show-off

with her best friend. "I know! I swear, I don't know how I pulled that off!"

"When did you find time to practice? Were you here over the weekend?"

"No, that's what's really unbelievable. I haven't practiced at all!"

But Coach Persky certainly thought she had, and for good reason. Amy found that she had improved considerably in other areas of gymnastics as well. Her tumbling was faster and neater, and for the first time ever she was able to keep her legs together when she swung around the uneven bars.

She could sense Coach Persky's eyes on her. His brow was puckered, and he was certainly watching her with more interest than usual. He didn't say much, but he did grant her a nod of approval at the end of the session. "Nice work," he grunted. Jeanine was livid.

Nancy Candler was waiting in the car out front when Amy and Tasha came out of the arena. Amy realized that another advantage of having a best friend was the fact that you didn't have to do your own bragging.

"Dr. Candler, you should have seen Amy in class today," Tasha announced from the backseat as soon as they were settled in the car. "She was great!"

Amy was too giddy with excitement to fake any modesty. "I really was, Mom. I did better than I've ever done before. Honestly, Mom, I was practically perfect!"

"Not just practically," Tasha interjected. "One hundred percent perfect!"

"Perfect?" Nancy echoed. She glanced briefly at Amy in the passenger seat and smiled, but Amy thought the smile seemed a little forced. She had to remind herself that it was her mother who always warned her about showing off.

"Not one hundred percent," Amy said hastily. "Coach Persky just said I've improved." She couldn't resist adding, "A lot." She wanted to go into the details, to tell her mother about the extraordinary vault and everything else, but her mother didn't ask any questions. Maybe she thought it would embarrass her in front of Tasha.

Back at the condo community, the girls separated to go to their respective homes. "How about macaroni and cheese for dinner?" Nancy asked as they went into the house.

Amy shrugged. "Sure, I don't care." She was a little annoyed that her mom still wasn't asking more questions about her gymnastic triumphs. She didn't seem the least bit excited.

Amy followed her mother into the kitchen. "Mom, did you do gymnastics when you were my age?"

"No, gymnastics weren't as popular back then as they are now."

"Did you do any kind of sports?"

Her mother was paying more attention to the cheese

40

she was grating than to Amy. "Just the usual schoolyard thing."

"What about my father? Was he athletic?"

There was a fraction of a pause in the grating. "No, not really."

"Because I think maybe I have talent, and I wonder who I got it from. Isn't that the kind of thing that's inherited from one of your parents?"

"Not necessarily." Amy waited for her to say more, but it was clear that Nancy had nothing to add on the subject. Amy gave up and went into the living room, where she looked under an end table. On a shelf was a large pink-and-white scrapbook that had been there forever. Amy dragged it out, sat on the rug, and opened it.

She'd looked at her baby book before, of course, but not with any particular need in mind. This time she examined the contents carefully, looking for something she'd be able to use in her autobiography.

There was a birth announcement, but it didn't tell her anything unusual or interesting—just her name, birth date, height, and weight. It didn't even give the name of the hospital where she was born. There were the usual pictures of a baby in a cradle. A lock of brown hair was taped to a page. Then there were the dates of her "firsts"—first step (thirteen months), first word ("Mama," sixteen months). More photos. More firsts—loss of first baby tooth, first report card. Absolutely nothing re-markable. It could have been anyone's baby book.

"Amy? Could you come in here and make a salad?"

Amy closed the book, put it back under the end table, and went into the kitchen. "Mom, I was born in Los Angeles, wasn't I?" she asked as she searched the refrigerator for salad stuff.

"Yes."

"What hospital?"

Her back to Amy, Nancy continued to grate cheese silently for a few seconds. "Why do you want to know that?"

Amy hesitated. For some reason—and she had no idea why—she didn't want to tell her mother about the assignment. "Just curious."

"I don't remember," her mother replied.

Amy was incredulous. "You don't remember what hospital you had a baby in?"

"Amy, it was a long time ago, and things were crazy. Your father had just died, there was the fire in our old house . . . besides, I think that hospital was torn down."

"Oh. Mom?"

"What?"

"Do I have a pediatrician?"

This time her mother actually turned around, and there was some alarm in her voice. "Why? Aren't you feeling well?"

"I feel fine," Amy assured her. "It's just that, well, Tasha was talking about her pediatrician today. And I don't remember ever going to one."

Nancy returned to grating. "Well, of course you had a pediatrician, when you were a baby. But . . . he died, and then you were so healthy, I never saw the need to find another doctor for you."

"But I've had vaccinations and checkups and all that?"

"Yes, of course."

"Then how come I don't remember ever having a checkup?"

"Because you were too young. Amy, why don't you start washing that lettuce?"

"But Tasha says she's had checkups every year, and she remembers getting shots and stuff."

Nancy's voice grew testy. "Amy, if you're not going to make a salad, then go set the table, or do something to help. I've got work to do after dinner."

It was becoming very clear to Amy that her mother would be no help whatsoever with this autobiography. Maybe Tasha was right—looking in her official school folder might be the only way she could get any information at all.

Okay, so it was against the rules. It wasn't all *that* terrible. Anyway, it was *her* folder. It wasn't like she was breaking into a bank.

"I'm here to see the director," the man said to the receptionist.

"Is he expecting you?" she asked.

"Yes."

The receptionist picked up the telephone and pressed a button. After a few words, she nodded to the man. He went into the office.

The director didn't rise from behind his desk, nor did he bother with greetings or a handshake—he never did. "Close the door," he said to the man. When that was done, he simply waited.

"I think I've found one of them," the man said.

"You think?"

"I don't have enough hard evidence to be sure."

"Photos?"

The man placed them on the desk. The director glanced at them briefly. "These are worthless. They tell us nothing."

"Yes, sir, I know."

There was a moment of silence.

"Continue surveillance," the director said. "Follow her, record all activities, including those that appear inconsequential. I'll expect a report on Wednesday."

The man nodded. "Yes, sir."

The director didn't rise; he didn't bother with good-byes. He never did.

four

When the doorbell rang the next morning, Amy had just started eating her cereal. She checked her watch. "Tasha's early," she said. "That's a switch."

But it wasn't Tasha at the door. "Hi, I'm Monica Jackson, your new neighbor."

Amy recognized the woman who had waved at Tasha yesterday. Today she looked a little more ordinary, in blue jeans and a T-shirt, but her hair was still red and wild. "Hi, I'm Amy Candler."

Nancy had obviously heard the strange voice. She hurried into the living room, wearing that nervous expression that had become all too familiar to Amy. "Yes?" she asked sharply.

The woman began to introduce herself again. "I'm Monica Jackson—" but Nancy didn't let her get any farther.

"Yes, what do you want?"

Amy was surprised. Her mother might not be the most outgoing person in the world, but she wasn't usually this rude. Monica, too, appeared to be taken aback by her tone. Her own voice became slightly frosty.

"Sorry if I'm disturbing you. I just moved in, around the corner, and I was wondering if you might have a hammer I could borrow."

Nancy visibly relaxed. "Oh. Of course. Please, come in. I think the hammer is in the kitchen."

Amy followed the new neighbor as she followed Nancy to the kitchen. "Excuse me if I was rude," Nancy was saying. "People have been coming to the door lately, trying to sell magazine subscriptions. I've learned that if you're just the least bit friendly, it's impossible to get rid of them."

"That's okay," Monica said. "Thanks for the warning."

Amy hadn't noticed any people coming by to sell anything recently. She figured they must come by after she left for school and before her mother left for the university where she taught.

In the kitchen, Nancy began opening drawers. "I know I've got tools in here somewhere."

Monica was looking around the room. "This is great. I love the way you've decorated the kitchen." Her eyes rested on the collection of photographs. She moved closer and began to study them. She picked one up. "Is this you?"

Nancy turned to look. It was the picture of her university graduation. "Yes, that's me," she said cautiously.

"I thought you looked familiar!" Monica exclaimed. "You went to UCLA, didn't you?"

"Yes." Nancy was still sounding cautious.

"So did I! I think we had a class together, sophomore year, or maybe it was junior year. Did you take Art of the High Renaissance, with Brentelli?"

"Yes, I did!"

Amy gaped. "Mom! You took art courses?"

"History of art," her mother said. "It was an elective. Believe it or not, Amy, I do have some interests outside of biology." She looked at Monica in a more direct and friendly way. "You know, I think I remember you. But something's different."

"My hair," Monica said. "It was long, brown, and straight. I ironed it daily so I could look like every other hippie."

"You ironed your hair?" Amy asked in disbelief.

"Ironic, isn't it? We thought we were free spirits, rebels against society. But we were still conformists, we just adopted a different set of status symbols." She looked at Nancy. "Flared jeans and leather sandals with straps that ran halfway up the leg, right?"

Nancy nodded. "Love beads and peasant blouses."

"Indian headbands, remember those?" Monica offered.

They both started laughing. Amy was floored.

"Mom! You never told me you were a hippie!"

"Well, I dressed like one," Nancy said. "What have you been doing since school, Monica?"

"I studied art in Paris, spent a couple of years in New York, and for the past fifteen years I've been working for an advertising agency in Chicago. I got sick of the snow, so I moved back out here."

"Do you have children?"

"No, and I never married. I paint, and I make jewelry. To pay the bills, I design covers for paperback novels. What have you been up to?"

"I got a doctorate at Berkeley, and I went to work in a research lab in Washington, D.C. Now I'm teaching biology at Southern California University. Here's the hammer."

"Thanks. Are you divorced?"

"No. Widowed."

"Oh." Monica replaced the photo of Nancy on the shelf. Then she gasped. "You married *him*?"

Amy was alarmed to see her mother go pale. "What?"

Monica had picked up the photo of Amy's father. "Isn't this Steve Anderson? He was two years ahead of us at UCLA?"

"You knew Steve?"

"Oh no, not really, I never even spoke to him. I just remember seeing him on campus."

Nancy's face began to return to its original color.

"Wait a minute," Amy interrupted. "Steve Anderson? I thought his name was Steve Candler."

"I kept my maiden name after I married," her mother told her. "Then, when you were born and Steve was . . . gone, I thought it would be less confusing if you had my last name."

"When did you two marry?" Monica asked.

"Oh . . . a while after graduation," Nancy said vaguely. "He died in an accident, before Amy was born."

"How sad. I'm truly sorry." Monica studied the photo. "He was awfully good-looking. I remember thinking that when I saw him on campus."

"Do you remember anything else about my father?" Amy asked eagerly.

"No," Monica said regretfully. "Like I said, I didn't actually know him."

The doorbell rang again. This time it was Tasha.

"Guess who's in our kitchen?" Amy greeted her as she stepped inside. "Monica, the artist! She was in school with my mother, and you're not going to believe this, she knew my father! Well, she didn't really know him, but she remembers seeing him around when she was at UCLA. Isn't that amazing? All she remembers is that he was really good-looking."

"That's nice," Tasha said, but it was clear to Amy she hadn't really been listening.

"What's the matter?"

Tasha spoke glumly. "It's Tuesday."

"So?"

"It's National Dental Week, remember?"

That wasn't the kind of event that Amy noted on her calendar, but she recalled seeing a poster in the girls' locker room in the gym. Still, she didn't understand what this had to do with Tasha's mood.

"So?"

"So this is the day they're giving the free dental exams in the cafeteria. And my mother says I have to get one, because our regular dentist moved away and I haven't had a checkup in eight months."

Amy didn't have to ask any more questions. Tasha's fear of dentists was well known to her. She tried to reassure her friend. "The dentist is just going to look in your mouth, Tasha. Even if he sees something wrong, he can't do anything right there at school. He'll just send a note home."

"Yeah, I know," Tasha said, her voice still grim. "And then my mother will take me to another dentist."

"Well, nothing's going to happen today, so don't worry about it now."

Tasha looked at her in despair. "But you know how I feel about dentists. What if I panic in the cafeteria? What if I freak out in front of everyone?"

"You won't do that," Amy said, trying to sound more confident than she felt.

"I might," Tasha said darkly. Then, after a moment, she asked, "Are you getting a checkup?"

"No."

"It's free," Tasha pointed out. "You don't even have to have a note from your parents."

"But I don't *need* a checkup," Amy said. "My teeth are fine."

"How do you know they're fine if you never have checkups? It wouldn't kill you to have one, you know." After a moment, she added, *"Please?"*

Amy sighed. "You really want me to have a checkup that I don't need, just so I can go there with you, is that it?"

"Yes."

"Okay," Amy said. "But then you owe me a favor."

"What?" Tasha asked.

"Help me get into my folder at school."

Tasha gasped. "Really? You'll do it?"

"If you'll come with me."

"Wow," Tasha breathed. "I've never broken a school rule before. Not a major one." She bit her lower lip. Then she grinned. "It's a deal."

Keeping her end of the bargain wasn't difficult at all for Amy. Students who were having dental checkups were excused from second-period classes. Waiting with a jittery Tasha in the cafeteria wasn't exactly fun, but it was better than sitting through geography.

The dentist was a nice man who allowed Amy to stay by Tasha's side while she had her exam. Tasha's eyes were squeezed shut, as if she was on the verge of screaming. But she didn't; she survived the exam, and the only bad moment came when the dentist made some ominous noises about Tasha's need to see an orthodontist.

Amy's exam took even less time. "Beautiful, beautiful," the dentist murmured as he admired the reflection in the little mirror he poked around her mouth. He proclaimed her teeth perfect, and even congratulated her on the care she obviously gave them.

Tasha was impressed. "How many times a day do you floss?" she asked Amy as they left the cafeteria.

"Just once," Amy admitted. "And I don't always remember."

"So your teeth are just naturally perfect," Tasha said. "Like everything else about you. You don't need glasses, you don't need braces, you don't have any allergies. . . . You'll probably go through your entire adolescence without getting a single pimple."

Amy wasn't listening. They were passing the bulletin board outside the principal's office and a notice had caught her eye. "Look."

Tasha read the notice out loud. " 'Faculty meeting

three-forty-five, media center.' " She realized the significance of this, and she went a little pale. Amy saw that and frowned.

"You're not going to bail out on me, are you?"

Tasha straightened her shoulders. "Absolutely not. It was my idea, remember? I'll meet you at your locker after last period."

Tasha may have been gutless when it came to dentists, but she was a loyal, true, and almost fearless friend. At 3:45, they were approaching the principal's office.

As Tasha had predicted, the office door was unlocked, and no one was inside. "I can't believe they leave it open like this," Amy murmured.

"Well, it's not like this is a bank, or a store," Tasha said. "There's nothing valuable in here."

"Except to me," Amy reminded her.

The file cabinets weren't locked either, and Tasha knew which ones held the student records. It was so easy. They opened the cabinet labeled A–C, and there they were, fat accordion folders arranged in alphabetical order by last names. Tasha watched the door while Amy flipped through the folders and read aloud the names on the tabs. "Caine, Callen, Cameron, Carlson . . ." She stopped. "I'm not here!"

"Keep looking," Tasha said. "Maybe it's out of order."

"No, wait, here it is," Amy said. It was right where it was supposed to be, between Cameron and Carlson.

But she could see why she'd missed it the first time. It wasn't like the others, thick with papers.

"It's empty!"

"That's impossible," Tasha said.

"See for yourself."

Reluctantly Tasha left her place by the door. Amy opened the brown folder bearing her name and let Tasha peer inside. She tried to come up with an explanation. "Maybe they're transferring the information to computers."

Amy went back into the drawer. She couldn't see any other empty folders. "Why would they start with mine?"

"I don't know."

"What are you doing?" said a sharp voice behind them. The girls froze. Slowly they turned around.

Amy didn't recognize the man who stood there. He was tall and slender, with dark, neatly combed hair, and he was dressed in a suit. Somebody's father, maybe?

He repeated his question. "What are you doing?"

"We were just looking for something," Tasha began, but Amy nudged her hard before she could say more. Didn't Tasha realize they were alone in this office with a total stranger? This man didn't look particularly dangerous, but they'd all been instructed since they were infants that bad guys didn't always look like bad guys.

The man stepped toward them. Amy and Tasha stepped back. "You come any closer, we're going to scream," Amy said, hoping the tremble in her voice didn't make her words less threatening. The man ignored her and took the empty folder out of her hand. He looked at the name on the tab. Then, slowly, his eyes moved up to Amy's face.

He didn't seem angry or even annoyed, just sort of curious and interested. And he kept his eyes on Amy as he replaced the file in its proper spot.

Then a small woman with steel-gray hair entered the office. "Mr. Devon," she began, and then she noticed Amy and Tasha. "What are you girls doing in here?"

Amy had always found the Parkside Middle School principal sort of intimidating. With the frown she wore now, Dr. Noble was downright scary. Frantically Amy tried to think of some logical explanation for their presence, but nothing came to her. She could only hope that Tasha, with her vivid imagination, would be able to make up a brilliant excuse.

But as it turned out, no excuse was necessary. The strange man answered for them.

"They wanted to see the lost-and-found box. One of them appears to have misplaced a . . . what was it? A watch?" He was still looking at Amy as he spoke, so Amy nodded.

"Yes," she said faintly, "a watch."

"And did you find your watch?" Dr. Noble asked.

"No."

The principal continued to frown. "You should be more careful with your possessions, young lady."

"Yes, Dr. Noble, I will."

Dr. Noble's nod told them they'd been dismissed. Together Amy and Tasha backed out of the office. They walked rapidly until they were outside, and then they broke into a run. Amy wanted to move a whole lot faster, but Tasha was holding her hand, so she had to keep pace.

They didn't stop running until the school was out of sight, and then they collapsed on someone's front lawn in hysterical giggles.

"I thought I'd die!" Tasha gasped. "Did your heart stop when you heard that man?"

Amy let out the breath she'd been holding for what felt like forever. "No kidding, I was totally freaked. And then when Dr. Noble came in, I didn't know if I should be glad or double-freaked."

"Who was that man anyway?"

"I don't know, I never saw him before. What did Dr. Noble call him?"

"Mr. Devon," Tasha answered. "It sounds sort of familiar."

The name was familiar to Amy too, and then she recalled where she'd heard it before. "The announcements this morning on the intercom, remember? He's the new assistant principal."

"Oh, yeah. What happened to Ms. Carroll?"

Amy shrugged. "I don't know."

Tasha started giggling again. "And you told the assistant principal if he came any closer you were going to scream!"

"Well, how was I supposed to know he was the assistant principal?" Amy retorted. "He could have been some kind of pervert looking for girls to kidnap."

"I think I'm going to like the new assistant principal a whole lot better than the old one," Tasha declared. "Can you believe how he didn't turn us in? He actually made up a story to protect us! Could you imagine that mean Ms. Carroll doing anything like that?"

"No." Amy pulled up a blade of grass from the lawn and began splitting it in half. "I wonder why he did that."

"I don't know and I don't care," Tasha stated. "I'm just glad he did. Do you have any idea how much trouble we could have been in if he'd told Dr. Noble we were looking in the files?"

They rose from the lawn and started walking toward home. "It's weird, though," Amy commented. "The assistant principal lying to the principal. Covering up for students. It doesn't make any sense."

"Maybe he's just nice," Tasha suggested. "Or he wants to be popular with the students."

"Yeah, maybe," Amy said doubtfully. Tasha's explanations weren't very convincing. But Amy didn't brood over it, since she had more important things to worry about. Like, what happened to her file at school? Why was she the only one with an empty folder?

And where was she going to get information for her autobiography?

f5ve

Waiting outside school Wednesday afternoon for their ride to gymnastics, Amy and Tasha were still talking about the new assistant principal.

"Did you see him today?" Amy asked.

"No, did you?"

Amy nodded. "Just now, when I was going to my locker."

"Did he say anything to you?"

"No. He looked straight at me, and he acted like he'd never seen me before."

"Weird," Tasha commented.

"No kidding," Amy agreed. "And you know what? He doesn't *look* like an assistant principal."

"What's an assistant principal supposed to look like?"

"Ordinary. Not like him. He doesn't act like an assistant principal either. Assistant principals aren't supposed to be mysterious."

"Speaking of mysterious," Tasha said, "did you tell your mother about your file?"

"No, how could I tell her my official school folder was empty? She'd want to know how I got my hands on it."

"So what are you going to do about your autobiography?"

"I don't know. Last night I asked my mother if I had any grandparents on my father's side. She said he was an orphan. Isn't that a weird coincidence, both of my parents being orphans?"

"What about brothers and sisters?"

"I guess he didn't have any. I can't ask my mother any more questions, she gets too upset."

At that moment Tasha's mother pulled up in the station wagon. "Mom, you're late," Tasha declared as the girls climbed in.

Mrs. Morgan just laughed. "If I were you, young lady, I wouldn't go around accusing anyone of being late. How many tardies have you accumulated this year at school?"

"None," Tasha replied. "So far."

From the backseat, Amy assured Tasha's mother. "She's doing a lot better this year, Mrs. Morgan."

"I certainly hope so," Mrs. Morgan sighed. "Tasha was ten days late being born, and she's been late for practically every appointment since."

"Oh, Mother," Tasha groaned.

Impulsively Amy leaned forward and spoke to Tasha's mother. "Mrs. Morgan, what hospital was Tasha born at?"

"Doctors' Memorial. Why?"

"Oh, no reason. I was wondering if you could remember."

"Of course I can remember! I can tell you everything about that day. The room number, the name of the doctor, everything. Mothers don't forget details like that."

Amy sank back in her seat. My mother did, she thought. Was her mother so different from other mothers?

Mrs. Morgan got them to the gym on time, so they were spared the wrath of Coach Persky. But Amy wasn't really looking forward to this session. After her unusual performance on Monday, Coach Persky was going to have high expectations, and Amy worried that she might not be able to meet them. She was still wondering if her fantastic vaults had been a fluke.

Jeanine had to be hoping that was true too. As they changed clothes in the locker room, she was watching Amy warily. It was a little unnerving, but there was no way Amy would let Jeanine freak her out. That was why she didn't flinch when Jeanine suddenly cried out, "Ooh, Amy, what's that gross thing on your back?"

"I don't have a gross thing on my back, Jeanine," Amy replied.

Jeanine came up closer behind her. "It's a big dark spot." She let out an exaggerated gasp of horror. "Amy Candler, did you get a tattoo?"

"No, Jeanine, I don't have a tattoo."

"Then maybe you're getting leprosy."

Tasha came to Amy's defense. "Don't be so stupid, Jeanine. It's just a birthmark."

Now Amy was puzzled. "I don't have a birthmark on my back."

"Sure you do," Tasha said. She instructed Amy to stand with her back to the mirror and look over her shoulder.

Something was definitely there. Amy stretched her hand to the spot on the upper right side of her back and rubbed it. It didn't feel like anything special, and it didn't hurt. But it didn't go away either.

"You better tell Coach Persky about that," Jeanine said. "You might not be fit to do gymnastics." With that she sauntered out of the locker room.

Amy continued to look at the mark on her back. It wasn't all that big, or dark, but it was definitely a mark.

And it wasn't just a spot, like Jeanine said. It had a shape—like a crescent moon. "What *is* that?"

"It's just a birthmark," Tasha assured her.

"A birthmark is something you're born with," Amy said. "I've never seen this before."

"You just haven't noticed it before," Tasha said.

"Have you see it before?"

"No," Tasha admitted. "But I don't usually pay that much attention to your back. It was probably always there, just smaller and lighter."

"But why would it change?" Amy asked.

"Puberty?" Tasha suggested. "Come on, we're going to be late."

Amy tried to put the birthmark or whatever it was out of her mind, but it wasn't easy. And now she knew she wouldn't do so well in class. Whenever she had something else on her mind, she couldn't concentrate.

The class was divided into three groups to rotate among the vault, the uneven bars, and the balance beam. Tasha was sent off to work on the beam. Amy was in the vault group, just behind Jeanine.

It was obvious that Jeanine had done some serious practicing since the last class. Even Amy had to admit that Jeanine performed her vault just as well as Amy had done hers on Monday. Coach Persky gave her one of his rare almost-smiles of approval.

It must have been her natural competitive spirit that spurred Amy on not only to equal Monday's vault but to exceed it. That was the only way she could explain the performance she gave after Jeanine's. Her run was faster, her jump off the board was higher, and she punched the horse with more energy than she'd ever had before. In the split second that she was in the air, she realized she had the power and height to do something extra before landing, so she went into a multiple twist.

Coach Persky didn't give her a smile. She got something better—a long, hard look and a slow nod. "Show-off," Jeanine hissed in her ear. Amy was too happy to care.

The uneven bars came next. This was Amy's fun event. She loved the swinging, the flying, the somer-saults and pirouettes. But her pleasure in doing the routine often kept her from concentrating sufficiently, and the coach often criticized her for being sloppy.

This time, though, it was so remarkably easy! The tingly thrill she'd experienced on Monday came flooding back, more tingly than before. Her whole body felt positively electric! She'd always loved gymnastics—but she'd never thought she could be this good at it.

Her routine got another nod from the coach and an evil eye from Jeanine. She didn't have much opportunity to revel in her success, however. She now had to go on the balance beam.

Practically every girl in the class was afraid of the balance beam, even Jeanine. It was like walking a tightrope. Amy's legs would tremble as she made her way across the beam, and she considered herself lucky if she got to the other end without falling off.

Everyone was quiet as Jeanine executed a nice mount and went into her beam exercises. Suddenly the silence was broken by Coach Persky's voice, louder than usual.

"Hey, you! Cut that out!"

The shock of the question sent Jeanine wavering, and she jumped off the beam before she could fall. The others turned to see what Coach Persky was talking about. He was already on the other side of the gym, approaching a man. A man who held a camera.

Amy caught her breath and looked around for Tasha. Tasha was watching Coach Persky too, but she didn't seem particularly bothered by what she saw. Didn't she recognize him? Amy wondered. Couldn't she see that the man Coach was approaching was the same man they'd seen taking pictures in front of their school? And the same man Amy saw—*thought* she saw—across the street from her house?

"What do you think you're doing?" Coach demanded. "You're not supposed to be in here."

The photographer didn't cringe. "I'm a freelance photographer," he explained. "I've got an assignment from *TeenSport* magazine, for an article on gymnastics."

"No one takes pictures of my girls without permission," Coach declared. "You're not even supposed to be in the sports center without authorization. Get out, now!"

So that explained why she kept seeing that guy around. He was just a pushy photographer for a popular magazine, a magazine Amy had read many times. There was nothing out of the ordinary going on at all.

"Coach should have made the guy give him the film," she commented to the gymnast standing by her.

"Why?" the girl asked.

"Because he's not supposed to be in here."

"Why not?"

"It's against the rules for anyone to be in here without authorization. You heard the coach."

"No, I didn't."

Amy frowned. "What do you mean, you didn't hear the coach?"

"How could anyone hear him?" the girl responded. "He's not *that* loud. And they're all the way on the other side of the gym."

"Well, *I* heard him," Amy said, and she considered suggesting to the girl that she get her hearing checked.

Tasha came over to her. "What was that all about?"

Amy was watching Coach Persky escort the man out of the building. "He was taking photos without permission." She turned to Tasha. "Didn't you hear Coach Persky?"

"No." She gazed at Amy in awe. "Wow, could you really hear them from this far away? That's amazing."

There was nothing amazing about it at all, Amy thought. The conversation between Coach Persky and the photographer had been perfectly clear. Tasha must have been daydreaming.

"He was the same man who was taking pictures at school," Amy added. "Didn't you recognize him?"

"No." Tasha couldn't say more because Coach Persky was returning and she had to scurry back to her own group. Jeanine went back up on the balance beam. The interruption must have unnerved her, because she didn't do so well. And then it was Amy's turn.

For once, she completed her mount on her first attempt. *That* was pretty remarkable. Then it occurred to her that the beam felt different today. No, *she* felt different. Suddenly, as if by magic, her fear was gone. Her feet gripped the beam tightly. She was strong and she moved with total assurance.

She executed a cartwheel, a handspring, a split, with precision and balance. She felt such exhilaration, such joy, that she wanted to do more, something different. Something she'd seen famous gymnasts do in world-class competitions—a back somersault. Was she crazy to try something she'd only seen on television? Probably. But she was feeling so good, so better than ever, so full of well-being and confidence—she knew she could do it.

So she did. She went into a back somersault, and then another, and then she surpassed her own dreams and dismounted with yet another back somersault. When her feet were about to hit the floor, she knew instinctively that her landing would stick, that she wouldn't falter. And her feet stuck as if they'd been slathered with glue.

She was beyond pleased with herself. She was ecstatic; she was on top of the world. The awed silence that greeted her performance indicated that everyone else was stunned too.

She didn't know what to expect from Coach Persky. Sometimes he could get really mad when the girls attempted something on their own, without training or practice. She turned uncertainly to face him.

He wasn't angry, that much was clear. There was a glint in his eyes that belied his stoic expression. But all he said was "See me after class, Amy."

That was enough to make Jeanine glare at Amy with even more hostility than usual. She didn't have a chance to say or do anything, though—after Coach Persky's end-of-class lecture on how lazy they all were, the class was dismissed.

"I'll meet you in the locker room," Amy told Tasha, and then she followed Coach Persky into his office.

Coach was brief and to the point. "I'm impressed with your performance lately," he told her. "It looks like you're developing some real expertise. I think we should begin thinking about competing."

Amy swallowed hard. "Competing?" she repeated faintly.

"It's been a while since I've seen a gymnast with natural skills like yours," the coach continued. "I think you've got real potential."

Amy's eyes widened. "Do you think I could make the national team?"

"Well, let's not get carried away," Coach Persky cautioned. "But . . . I wouldn't say that's out of the question. Let's start off with some additional training. Tell your mother to call me and we'll set up a schedule."

"I will," Amy said. "Thank you."

When she burst into the locker room, all the other girls looked up expectantly. Amy didn't keep them in suspense. She tried to keep her voice under control, but she wasn't very successful.

"He thinks I've got talent," she practically shrieked. "He wants me to take extra classes. He thinks maybe I could make the national team!"

She got the reaction she expected—gasps, a whoop or two, and a general squeal of congratulations. Only Jeanine said nothing. The jealousy in her expression was so apparent that Amy almost felt sorry for her.

It was great having a friend like Tasha, who wasn't the least bit jealous, just happy and excited for Amy. Even

Tasha's mother was excited to hear the news when she picked them up.

"I can see it now," Mrs. Morgan declared with gusto. "Amy at the Olympics! Amy scoring a perfect ten! Amy on the cover of a cereal box!"

Amy grinned. It was clear where Tasha got her wild imagination from. Still, it wasn't a bad fantasy, not at all.

"This calls for a celebration," Mrs. Morgan continued. "How about some ice cream?"

"Yes!" Tasha exclaimed. Then she turned to Amy. "Unless you want to get right home to tell your mother."

"She won't be home from the university for another hour at least," Amy said.

So they stopped at the place where they could get their favorite, soft vanilla ice cream dipped in chocolate, before they went home. Amy was still licking drops of chocolate from her cone when Mrs. Morgan dropped her off.

"See you tomorrow!" Amy called to Tasha. "Thanks for the ride and the ice cream, Mrs. Morgan."

She knew her mother hadn't returned yet, because the mail hadn't been picked up. Envelopes and catalogs were sticking out of the box by their door. Amy took the stuff out and went inside.

She dropped the mail on the coffee table and then went through it quickly to see if there was anything for her. There rarely was, except for a *Teen* magazine once a month and an occasional birthday-party invitation.

But today was different. There *was* an envelope with her name on it. Whose birthday was coming up? she wondered as she tore it open.

It wasn't a party invitation. Inside the envelope was a single white sheet of paper with three typed lines on it.

```
It is in your best interest to keep your
talents to yourself.
You may be in danger.
```

She stared at the words and read them over again. Then she looked at the envelope. There was no return address. There wasn't even a stamp. Someone had put this note in her mailbox.

It's a joke, she told herself. Someone's playing a game, someone's teasing me. It's a prank, just a joke. But as she read the lines over once again, she didn't feel like laughing.

A my lay flat on her bed and stared up at the ceiling. She turned to look at the clock by her bed and was dismayed to see that only two minutes had passed since she'd last looked. She got up and went to the window, but there was no sign of her mother's car.

She couldn't remember ever being so anxious to see her mother. But then, she'd never had so much to tell her before. She stuck her hand in her jeans pocket, pulled out the note, and read it again for the zillionth time.

```
It is in your best interest to keep your
talents to yourself.
You may be in danger.
```

Was it a threat? Who would want to threaten her? And what were these so-called talents she was supposed to have?

It hit her. Gymnastics! Today she had demonstrated a real talent for gymnastics. And then she knew who'd written the note.

This was just the kind of thing Jeanine would do. She had seen Amy's performance in class, and she had seen how Amy had suddenly improved. Amy was way beyond her now, and she was jealous. Since there was no way Jeanine could perform better than Amy, this was her way of making Amy stop showing how good she could be. And because they'd gone out for ice cream after gymnastics, there had been time for Jeanine to come by and stick the note in the mailbox.

It was so logical, so obvious. Now that she'd figured it out, she could smile. Did Jeanine really think she could scare her off so easily? Amy wasn't going to confront Jeanine with the note; she'd only deny it, so there was no point. She crumpled it up and tossed it across the room toward the wastebasket. The note dropped in cleanly. Her aim was definitely improving too.

Well, that was one less subject to discuss with her mother. But there was still that mark on her back. She stood with her back to her mirror, pulled up her T-shirt, and looked over her shoulder. It was still there, the small, dark crescent moon. Maybe it had been there forever and she just hadn't noticed it. After all, when was the last time she'd looked at her naked back?

Or maybe it did have something to do with puberty. All the magazines she read talked about teenagers getting spots. She knew they were referring to pimples, not crescent moons, but maybe this was just another kind of pimple. She decided to ignore it for the moment. Besides, what would her mother do if she told her about it. Take her to a doctor? That wasn't a very appealing notion. She'd never been to a doctor in her life, and she didn't want to start going now.

She let her T-shirt drop. Okay, she wouldn't mention this to her mother either. So now she had nothing but good news to report. And now she was even more anxious for her mother to come home.

She heard the car approach, and she was at the front door when her mother opened it. "Hi, Mom! Guess what I did in gymnastics today?"

"What?"

"A triple back flip!"

"Congratulations! I have no idea what a triple back flip is, but it certainly sounds impressive." Amy's mother started toward the kitchen, and Amy followed her.

"Coach Persky was definitely impressed. He wants you to call him to arrange for me to have extra sessions with him. Private sessions!"

"More classes?" Her mother began preparing coffee. "I didn't know you were getting that enthusiastic about gymnastics."

"I didn't know I could be this good!"

Nancy took a mug out of the cabinet. "Do you really want to put more time into gymnastics?"

"Coach says I have to, if I want to get into serious competition."

"Competition?" Nancy picked up the coffeepot to pour.

She wasn't getting it. She didn't understand the significance of what Amy was telling her. "Mom, I've got talent! And that's not just my opinion. Coach Persky said so, and he never gives out compliments. You should have seen me today! I was doing moves we haven't even practiced in class, moves I'd only seen on TV. It was weird. I don't know how I knew how to do them, but I did, and I did them perfectly. Mom, watch out!"

Nancy was staring at Amy, and the coffee was pouring over the side of the mug. As the hot liquid splashed on her hand, Nancy cried out and put the pot down.

"Are you okay?" Amy asked.

Nancy ran some cold water into the sink, letting it fall on her hand. "I'm fine," she said, but to Amy her voice sounded a little shaky. "Let's sit down." Gingerly she took her coffee cup to the kitchen table; Amy sat down next to her.

"I guess you must be pretty shocked by all this," Amy said. "It was a shock to me too. Mom, it was incredible! It was like, all of a sudden, out of nowhere, I could do anything. And I haven't even been practicing. Can you imagine how good I could be if I really started working at it? I could be a world-famous gymnast!"

Nancy didn't respond. She hadn't touched her coffee.

"Mom, are you sure you're okay? You look a little pale."

"I'm fine, Amy. Tell me exactly what happened in gymnastics today. Tell me everything; don't leave out any details." The seriousness of her expression was startling, but at least she seemed to be realizing how important this was. In detail, Amy described each skill she'd performed at a level beyond her wildest imagination.

"You should have seen Coach Persky's face. He was positively stunned!" The memory made her smile. "It's funny . . . I used to be so scared on the balance beam. But this time I wasn't scared at all. I knew I wouldn't fall."

"How did you know that?"

"I don't know. I just knew!" Amy giggled. "Sounds crazy, doesn't it?"

"That was the first time you felt like this?"

"Yeah. Well, on Monday, I did this perfect vault, better than I've ever done before, but I thought it was just a fluke. Today I did everything perfectly, and I know it wasn't a fluke. I can do it all again, just as well, maybe even better. I know I sound really conceited, but it's the truth, Mom. Do you believe me?"

"Yes," Nancy said. "I believe you."

Those were the words Amy wanted to hear, but her mother wasn't saying them right. Her tone wasn't excited at all. She sounded flat, hollow, as if Amy was telling her bad news instead of thrilling news. Maybe she was still in a state of shock.

"Anyway, Coach Persky wants me to start entering competitions. He thinks maybe I could make the national team. You know what that means? I could go to the Olympics!" Amy giggled. "Mrs. Morgan said she expects to see my face on a cereal box. I wonder if I get to choose which kind of cereal. I don't care, as long as it's not raisin bran—yuck."

Her mother didn't laugh. She didn't say anything. She seemed to be looking past Amy, at nothing in particular. She wasn't excited; she didn't even smile.

"Mom! Are you listening to me?"

"Yes, I'm listening." It was then that Amy noticed her mother was gripping the coffee mug so tightly that her knuckles were white. "Amy, can we discuss this later? I have a splitting headache."

That explained her strange behavior. "Okay," Amy said. "There's nothing to discuss, though. You just need to call Coach Persky tomorrow, okay?"

Her mother finally released the coffee mug, stood up, and walked to the window. With her back to Amy, she said, "No, I don't think so."

"Huh?"

"I don't want you getting into gymnastics competition."

"Why not?"

"Because . . . because I don't approve of competition among young people."

"Since when?" Amy wanted to know. "You were perfectly happy about my winning that spelling bee last year."

"That's different; that was school." Her mother turned and faced her. "I've read what happens to these young girls who get involved in gymnastics. It's not good for them. It takes up a lot of time, they miss out on too much. They get injured, they develop eating disorders."

"Not all of them," Amy protested. "Just the ones in those TV movies. Plenty of gymnasts are perfectly happy. And you only get injured when you do something wrong. I won't do anything wrong."

Nancy was shaking her head. "I'm sorry, Amy. I just don't want to take any chances. I can't allow this."

"But, Mom!"

Pain crossed her mother's face, but she continued to shake her head. "I'm not going to change my mind, Amy!" She turned and walked rapidly out of the kitchen.

Amy was too stunned to move. But after the immediate shock had passed, she was furious. How could her mother do this to her? How could she forbid her to do gymnastics when she could become a champion? Here she had suddenly developed a real talent, and her mother was going to toss it away. She was destroying her future! Amy was not going to let this happen; she wasn't giving up her chance at fame and glory and gold medals, not without a fight.

She went to the stairs. "Mom!" There was no answer. She ran upstairs and saw that her mother's bedroom door was closed. There were strange noises coming from the room. It took her only a few seconds to identify them.

Her mother was crying. Not wailing, not sobbing, just weeping softly.

Amy's anger faded. Now she was bewildered. She couldn't remember ever hearing her mother cry before. She'd seen her upset, sure, and distracted, and worried about stuff she never discussed with Amy. But Nancy Candler was not the kind of person who burst into tears easily. Amy went back downstairs to the kitchen, sat at the table, and pondered this.

Why would her mother get so upset? Did she really believe that Amy was on the verge of an eating disorder, or about to break every bone in her body? She was a scientist, for crying out loud, not the kind of person who had wild fears and fantasies.

Something else had to be bothering her. Something at work maybe. Amy glanced at the door that led into her mother's office and wondered if a clue to her mother's behavior might lie in there. She didn't dare go in to explore—the office was the one room in the house that was off limits to her, and to anyone else for that matter. Sometimes Amy thought her mother's greatest fear was finding a file folder out of order.

Or maybe her mother was having personal problems. That was hard to believe, since she didn't have much of a personal life. She never went out on dates. She didn't even have many friends.

That could be the problem, Amy thought. Her mother had to be lonely. Her life centered around her work and her daughter, and that must be why she didn't want Amy getting into gymnastics competitions. It would mean hours of practice, and traveling, and she probably thought it would take Amy away from her.

This was definitely not the time to nag her about calling Coach Persky. But Amy thought her mother really needed to get a life. If she had more friends of her own, maybe she wouldn't be so protective of Amy. She needed someone to hang out with, someone her own age. Someone like their new neighbor, Monica.

Monica . . . she seemed like the kind of person who knew how to have fun. And she even had something in common with Nancy, the same university. Yes, she was definitely a potential friend for Amy's mother. And there was no time like the present to get the friendship started, especially if Amy wanted her mother to call Coach Persky before too long.

But she couldn't just pop over to Monica's and ask her to be friends with her mother. She needed an excuse to visit, to start a conversation . . . the hammer! She could tell Monica she needed the hammer the neighbor had borrowed yesterday.

Amy could hear her mother upstairs still sobbing. Amazing. She could hear her all the way down here. But this was not the time to congratulate herself on her remarkable hearing. She slipped out of the house and went next door.

Monica answered the door immediately, and she looked pleased to see Amy. "Hi, come on in!"

The house Amy entered was structured exactly like Amy's, but all resemblance ended with the location of the walls and the placement of the stairs. Monica apparently had a passion for red and purple—the living room vibrated with color. Bright patterned rugs were scattered along the floors, and the walls were covered with paintings, collages, and unusual embroideries.

"Wow," Amy said. "Did you make all these paintings?"

"Some of them," Monica said. She pointed out the ones she'd painted. "The others were done by friends of mine."

"I'll bet you have lots of friends," Amy said.

Monica smiled. "That's one of the reasons I moved back to this area. Friends are awfully important, aren't they?"

Amy nodded. "I wish my mother had more friends. I think she's lonely."

That led easily into Amy's telling Monica about her mother's recent overprotectiveness, her moodiness, her strange reaction to Amy's gymnastics talent. Monica seemed to understand.

"Empty-nest syndrome," she pronounced it. "That usually doesn't happen till the child leaves home for college, but I guess you and your mother are closer than most."

"I'm glad we're close," Amy said. "I just wish she could be close to someone else once in a while. So she's not always worrying about me."

Monica looked thoughtful. "You know, I go to a lot of gallery openings, museum shows, that sort of thing.

Do you think she'd be interested in coming along sometime?"

She had Amy's undying gratitude. Amy didn't even have to pretend she needed the hammer back. Monica understood completely, and she promised to invite Nancy out very soon. Amy returned home in an optimistic mood.

It didn't last long. When she opened the door, Nancy came out of the kitchen. She wasn't crying anymore. Now she was angry.

"Amy, where have you been?"

"Just next door at Monica's."

"Don't ever run off like that without telling me where you're going!"

Amy had never before heard such a combination of fear and fury in her mother's voice. At first she was too astonished to speak. Then the injustice of it all brought on her own fury.

"For crying out loud, Mom, what is your problem? I don't know what's bothering you, but you don't have to take it out on me!"

"I just want to know where you are at all times," her mother declared.

"At all times? Good grief, I'm not a baby! Mom, what's gotten into you lately? And why won't you let me take private gymnastics lessons and start competing?"

Her mother seemed to be making an effort to calm

herself. "Amy, please. Don't ask so many questions. I know what's best for you."

With that unsatisfactory explanation, she turned away, went into her office, and shut the door. Amy stared at the closed door and began to wonder if she just might be able to get up the nerve to break another rule.

"The director is expecting you," the receptionist said, and she pressed the button that opened the office door. The investigator went in.

"Do you have anything?" the director asked.

"Yes."

The director scanned the report. He took the photos from the folder and examined them. "She has a mark."

"It could be a natural birthmark," the investigator said, "but that would be highly coincidental. The performance in gymnastics is interesting."

The director put the report and the photos back into the folder. "It's a beginning. But we need more definitive evidence."

"What do you suggest?"

"A hair sample."

The man agreed.

seven 7

"I don't get it," Tasha said as they walked to school the next day. "You'll eat anything that doesn't eat you first. And your mother doesn't want you to be a gymnast because she thinks you'll get an eating disorder?"

"That was one reason," Amy said glumly. "The others were pretty feeble too. They're all just excuses, Tasha. There's got to be another reason, a real reason."

"Why would she keep the real reason a secret?"

"Who knows? But I don't think it has anything to do with gymnastics. She's turning into a nervous wreck. Today she wanted to drive me to school! I talked her out of it, but I'll bet she calls the school to see if I arrived safely."

Tasha was impressed. "Geez, Amy. She's always been kind of overprotective, but this is getting ridiculous."

Amy agreed. "It's as if she's afraid to let me out of her sight, like something terrible is going to happen to me."

"Something like what?"

"I don't know. Maybe she thinks I'll be hit by a car or struck by lightning. Or I'll get in a car with a stranger and be kidnapped. You should have seen her yesterday, when I got back from Monica's." The memory of her mother's hysterics made her shake her head. "Something's going on, Tasha. She's got a secret."

"All mothers keep secrets," Tasha assured her. "Like, I asked my mother why my cousin Ellen got divorced after only three months of being married. I know it had to be something pretty bad because everyone was whispering about it. But all she would tell me is that Ellen didn't really know the man she married. I'm still trying to figure out what that means."

"Well, I want to know what's going on," Amy said. "If it's got something to do with my father, I think I have a right to know."

Tasha gasped. "I just had an idea. What if he's alive, and she's afraid he's going to kidnap you?"

That sounded awfully far-fetched to Amy, but she was willing to consider anything. "Why would my mother keep that a secret from me?"

"There are a zillion possibilities," Tasha said excitedly.

"Like, he could be a criminal. Or an alcoholic or a drug addict or something like that. No offense," she added hastily.

Amy didn't feel offended. Maybe she should be. After all, Tasha was suggesting that her blood relation, her true biological father, was a bad person. But she couldn't admit to having any real sense of attachment to him. It was hard to imagine him being alive. She didn't think he could be alive.

"Are you going to look for him?"

"I could try. I've seen those ads on the Internet, where they find missing people."

"You'd better get right to work if you're going to find him in time," Tasha advised.

"In time for what?"

"To get information before your autobiography's due."

Amy had almost forgotten about the assignment. She was going to have to take some sort of action right away. With this in mind, she went to homeroom early, before the bell, to talk to her English teacher.

"Ms. Weller?"

The teacher looked up. "Yes, Amy?"

"I'm having a problem with my autobiography."

"What kind of problem?"

"I don't know anything about myself."

Ms. Weller's brow puckered. "I don't understand, Amy. What do you mean?"

"My father's dead, and my mother says she's forgotten a lot. I don't have any grandparents or relatives to ask. My mother doesn't like to talk about the past. She gets upset. I can't even find out where I was born!"

"Well, that shouldn't be too hard to learn. It would be on your birth certificate."

"But I can't find my birth certificate!" Amy said helplessly.

Ms. Weller thought. "There should be a copy in your file here at school. Why don't you ask the secretary for a copy?"

"It wouldn't do any good," Amy said.

"Why not?"

"Because it's not there."

Ms. Weller's eyebrows went up. "Are you sure? How do you know that?"

Amy flushed. This was her favorite teacher. It wouldn't be easy to lie to her, and Amy didn't want to anyway. "I looked in my folder," she confessed. "It was empty."

Ms. Weller didn't ask how Amy had got her hands on her folder. "Empty! That's not possible. If you scrape your knee, they put a note in those folders."

"I've never scraped my knee," Amy said.

"Well, even so . . ." Ms. Weller looked at her watch. "We have a few minutes before the bell. Let's go to the office." On the way there, she added, "Even if your birth certificate is missing from the file, all you have to do is write to the state health department and they'll send you a copy."

The main office of the school was busy and noisy, with teachers chatting and checking their mailboxes and students dropping off absentee excuses and other stuff. Amy was only vaguely aware of the activity around her. Her eyes locked on the man in the doorway of the assistant principal's office.

Mr. Devon wasn't doing anything; he just stood there. Amy followed Ms. Weller to the desk. "Ms. Rankin? I need Amy Candler's file."

The secretary went to the file cabinet and opened a drawer. "Let's see, Candler . . . yes, here we are." Then she pulled out a folder that was just as fat as everyone else's and handed it to Ms. Weller.

"Are you sure that's mine?" Amy asked.

Ms. Weller nodded as she looked over a note. "I see you won the school spelling bee last year." She flipped through the papers. "Your report cards, your standardized test results . . . here are your vaccination records . . . ah!" She took a sheet and handed it to Amy. "A copy of your birth certificate." She went back to the desk. "Ms. Rankin, could I have a photocopy of this?"

She returned a moment later, replaced the certificate in the folder, and handed Amy the copy. "I need to get back to homeroom, Amy. You've got two minutes before the bell." Ms. Weller left the office, and Amy devoted her attention to the paper.

It looked authentic. There was a seal from the State of California, and plenty of signatures and numbers. And the information it revealed was correct. There was her name, her date of birth, and even her time of birth. (That was an unexpected bonus—now she could send off for one of those astrological charts that were advertised in the back of some of her favorite magazines.) There was Amy's mother's name, birth date, and social security number, and the same information about Amy's father. But no grandparents were listed, and no other relatives either.

There *was* a hospital name, though—Eastside General. And the doctor who delivered her had signed the certificate. His scrawl was practically illegible. Fortunately the name was typed underneath the signature: J. R. Jaleski, M.D.

She tried to recall whether she'd ever heard that name before, but it didn't ring any bells. There was definitely an Eastside General, though—she'd even been there once, two years ago, visiting a classmate with a broken leg. She hadn't felt any sort of attachment to the place, but of course, she hadn't known then what she knew now. Still, she should have sensed something special about the hospital.

She was sensing something right now. A feeling of being watched . . . She raised her eyes.

Mr. Devon was still in his doorway, and he was looking at her. No, he wasn't just looking—he was studying her, scrutinizing her, like something under a microscope. Was it just her imagination that he gave an almost imperceptible nod?

He was probably warning her that the bell was about to ring. She folded the paper, stuck it in her pocket, and left the office.

"So why was the folder empty before?" Tasha asked as they left the building after their last class.

"Who knows?" Amy replied. "Maybe all the papers fell out. It doesn't matter. It looks just like everyone else's now."

"Did you see your birth certificate?"

"Yeah, I got a copy." Amy fished it out of her pocket and gave it to Tasha.

Tasha looked it over. "It looks like an ordinary birth certificate."

"Of course it's ordinary. What did you expect?"

Tasha grinned. "Oh, I don't know, maybe a special citation. World's most perfect baby, that sort of thing."

"Ha, ha," Amy retorted. She looked at her watch. "I wonder if Coach Persky has a class this afternoon."

"Why?"

"I was thinking about calling him at the sports center and asking him if he'd call my mother. Since my mother isn't going to call him."

Tasha looked at her quizzically. "You really want to get into heavy-duty competition? You never talked about wanting to be a serious gymnast before."

Amy shrugged. "I didn't know I had the talent. But if I'm as good as Coach Persky says, I might as well go for it."

"It's not fair," Tasha sighed. "You're good at everything."

"That's not true," Amy argued.

"Oh, come on, think about it. Remember when we were in chorus last year? And the director said you had perfect pitch? And last summer, when we took those swimming lessons at the Y? The teacher said your swan dive was absolutely perfect, remember?"

"Knock it off," Amy said sharply.

"Hey, I'm giving you compliments!"

Amy frowned. "I don't want people talking about me like that. I'll get a reputation for being a goody-goody. Little Miss Perfect."

"I'm sure you'll find something you can't do perfectly," Tasha assured her. "Eventually."

"Yeah," Amy said. "Like writing this autobiography. I can tell you right now, *that's* not going to be perfect."

"Well, at least you've finally got some information," Tasha said.

"But not much," Amy replied. "Not enough. I've got my height and weight, the name of the hospital where I was born, and the doctor who delivered me. I don't think I'll be able to get ten pages out of that."

"Write about how you want to be a gymnastics champion," Tasha suggested.

"No way," Amy declared. "We have to present these reports orally too. I can't talk about how perfect my vaults are in front of the whole class. Especially when Jeanine is in the class."

Thinking about the assignment was putting her in a bad mood.

Tasha noticed. "Come on over to my place," she said. "Dad made a cheesecake for dessert last night, and there's half of it left—if my brother hasn't inhaled it yet."

Eric was outside on the driveway, shooting hoops with a friend. "Either the cheesecake's gone or he's forgotten about it," Tasha said. They were in luck. When they opened the refrigerator in Tasha's kitchen, they saw the cheesecake in all its creamy pale-yellow glory. Tasha brought it out to the table along with plates and forks.

"Mmm, this is fantastic," Amy said as she wolfed hers down and helped herself to seconds.

"And you won't even gain an ounce from it," Tasha complained. "I can practically feel myself expanding. You're so lucky."

"I'm lucky? With *my* mother? You're the one with the perfect mother."

Mrs. Morgan came into the kitchen. "Why, thank you, Amy. How would you girls like to go to the mall?"

"You see?" Amy said to Tasha. "Is that perfect or what?"

"Go get your brother," Mrs. Morgan instructed Tasha. "He needs shoes."

The girls went outside to the carport. Eric's friend had left, but Eric was still throwing the basketball. They watched as it hit the rim of the hoop. In his next effort, it hit the backboard and bounced off. It rolled to the end of the carport, where Amy picked it up.

Eric put out his hands. "Throw it," he ordered her. She did, but not in his direction. She aimed at the basketball hoop. The ball soared through the air, higher and farther, and it dropped cleanly through the net.

"Wow!" Tasha exclaimed.

Eric was staring at her, his mouth half-open. "Beginner's luck," he said finally. "You can't do it again."

"Oh, yeah? Give me the ball." Eric did. She aimed and threw the ball, and it cleared the net again. She'd known it would.

She grinned proudly until she noticed the way Eric was gaping at her. Her smile faded. This was exactly what she didn't want, someone looking at her like that, thinking she did everything better than anyone else. It was exactly what she'd told Tasha she was afraid of—

being a show-off, someone who would be disliked because she did things too well.

"Second-time luck," she said weakly.

They had to clear out of the driveway at that moment because Mrs. Morgan was backing the car out. Amy and Tasha sat in the back while Eric got into the front seat. He twisted around to face Amy. "Where did you learn to throw like that?" he demanded.

Amy gave him a helpless shrug.

"I've never seen a girl throw a ball as far as that," he said. "I've never seen a *boy* throw like that."

"Oh, come on, don't exaggerate," Amy remonstrated. "On TV I've seen Michael Jordan throw a ball from three times that distance."

"Well, sure," Eric said. "He's a grown man. I'm talking about a guy my age. Or an eleven-year-old girl."

"I happen to be twelve," Amy informed him. His gaze was making her more uncomfortable than Mr. Devon's at school. Maybe that was because she didn't have a super-secret longtime crush on Mr. Devon.

"Eric, fasten your seat belt," Mrs. Morgan ordered, and that put an end to his scrutiny. She drove out of the condo community and headed toward the freeway.

"You can't get on the freeway up there, Mrs. Morgan," Amy said. "There's a detour."

"Are you sure, Amy?" Mrs. Morgan asked. "The entrance was clear yesterday."

"There's a sign at the turnoff," Amy said. "It says Entrance Closed, Use Detour. See?"

"How could I possibly read a sign that's over a mile away?" Then, after a second, Mrs. Morgan asked, "How can *you* read a sign that's over a mile away?"

"Because she's got perfect eyesight," Tasha answered. "Like everything else. Perfect hearing, perfect teeth . . ."

"*I* have twenty-twenty vision," Mrs. Morgan said, "and I can't read the sign." But after another half minute of driving, she said, "Now I can." She turned off onto a side road. "Amy, you couldn't possibly have seen that sign from back there."

"She must have known it was coming up, and she just imagined she was actually reading it," Eric told his mother.

"No, I didn't," Amy protested.

Mrs. Morgan supported her. "She couldn't have seen it before, Eric, it wasn't there yesterday. But I still don't understand how you could have seen it from so far away, Amy."

Despite his seat belt, Eric was trying to twist around to get a look at Amy again. Amy pretended to be looking at something out the window. Now Eric had to be thinking she was some sort of Little Miss Perfect Goody-Goody Show-off Freak.

She saw another sign up ahead that interested her. It was close enough that she felt pretty sure everyone else could see it, so she pointed it out. "That's Eastside General Hospital. I was born there."

"Is there a plaque on the door?" Eric asked.

"What do you mean?"

"You know, a sign that says something like The Great Amy Candler Was Born Here."

"Very funny," Amy muttered, sinking back into her seat.

"Eric, don't tease," Mrs. Morgan reprimanded mildly. She slowed the car to a stop at a red light, just in front of the hospital.

"Amy," Eric said, "didn't you say you're twelve?"

"Yeah, why?"

"Then you couldn't have been born at Eastside General."

"Why not?"

"Look."

She sat forward and looked out the window at the sign in front of the hospital. It proclaimed the name of the hospital and the date it had been founded.

Two years *after* Amy was born.

eight 8

On the way home from the mall, the car passed East-side General again. Amy couldn't resist taking another look at the sign. Maybe they'd all read it wrong. But it was the same sign, and it presented the same date.

"Maybe there's another Eastside General," Tasha suggested.

Amy shook her head. "I don't think so."

"Then it's just a mistake on your birth certificate," Tasha said. "Someone typed the wrong hospital name."

Eric had another suggestion. "Or maybe your birth date's wrong, and you're really only ten."

He was teasing again, but she knew he was doing it to make her laugh. She could only manage a smile.

"I'm sure there's a perfectly logical explanation," Mrs. Morgan said. "Don't worry about it."

Tasha agreed. "What does it matter where you were born anyway? You're here now, that's what counts."

"Yeah, I guess," Amy said. She honestly didn't know why this was bothering her so much. Probably because there was still the autobiography to consider. Now she had one less bit of information she was sure of.

Mrs. Morgan dropped her off in front of her house, and she stopped at the mailbox. There was only one item inside—a long, plain white envelope. It was addressed to her, and there was no return address. Another message from Jeanine? Maybe Amy should inform her rival about her mother's decision regarding Amy's future in gymnastics. Then Jeanine wouldn't have to bother writing nasty notes.

She ripped the envelope open and pulled out the sheet of paper.

Congratulations, Amy Candler! It is our pleasure to inform you that you have won third prize in the Sunshine Square Annual Lottery. Your prize is a complimentary cut and styling at Hair Is Us, Sunshine Square's finest beauty salon.

```
Please call this number to make your
appointment.
```

She fingered a lock of her hair. A new hairstyle . . . it wasn't something she could write about in an autobiography, but it might lift her spirits.

Inside the house, she went upstairs to her room and turned on her computer. Quickly she typed up a letter to the California Department of Health requesting a copy of her birth certificate. Then she got on the Internet, accessed a search engine, and clicked on Directory Assistance. There she found several Missing Persons sites.

The first one sounded promising: "Looking for someone? Your first love, your favorite teacher, a distant relative you haven't seen in years? We can help you track this person down!"

She clicked on that site and was immediately presented with an elaborate application. It asked a million questions about the person she was seeking. She could only answer a few, and she couldn't even answer those completely. She knew his date of birth, but she didn't know where he was born. She knew where he went to college, because it was the same university her mother had attended, but she didn't know the year he graduated. She knew he had been in the army, but she didn't know what year he joined or what his ranking was. Based on the one and only photo she'd seen, she could provide hair and eye color, but she didn't know his height or weight or whether he had any distinguishing characteristics, like a scar or tattoo. All in all, it wasn't much, and she entered the application without much hope.

Then she gazed at the blank screen and wondered if she was wasting her time. Tasha had an incredibly wild imagination. Should Amy give her latest theory that her father was alive and wanted to kidnap her any real consideration? But there had to be some explanation for her mother's strange, secretive behavior.

She wasn't about to give up on asking her mother questions, but she knew she had to be more subtle in her approach, or Nancy would just get angry or start crying. Amy wouldn't mention the mistake on her birth certificate or her search for her father.

When her mother arrived home from work, Amy bounced down the stairs and greeted her with a cheery expression. "Hi, Mom, how was your day?"

Her mother smiled tiredly. "Long and boring. I attended a three-hour faculty meeting where nothing happened, and I gave a two-hour exam where all I could do was sit and listen to students groaning and moaning. How was your day?"

"Fine," Amy said, and brought the subject back

to Nancy. "Don't you like teaching at the university anymore?"

"Oh, I like teaching all right. I just wish I had better students and less paperwork."

Amy followed her into the kitchen, where Nancy went through her usual ritual coffee preparation. "Have you ever thought about going back into research?"

"What?"

"You told Monica you worked in a research laboratory in Washington, D.C., before I was born. Do you ever want to go back to doing that?"

Her mother seemed unusually intent on watching the drops of coffee pass through the filter. "No."

"What kind of research was it anyway?"

There was a moment of silence. "Biological research. Very complicated. I don't think you could understand it at your age."

"Try me," Amy said. "I'm getting smarter all the time."

Her mother gazed at her steadily, almost sadly. "Are you?"

"Sure, everything's changing about me," Amy said. "Puberty, remember?"

Nancy seemed to relax. "How could I forget?"

"I think it's time to change my hairstyle too," Amy went on. "Look at this. I won a free haircut." She dug into her pocket and showed her mother the announcement.

Nancy studied it. "What's the Sunshine Square Annual Lottery?"

"Some sort of contest, I guess." Amy opened the refrigerator and scanned the contents. "Are there any brownies left?"

"You entered a contest?"

"I must have. How else could I win third prize?"

"But you don't remember entering it."

"Huh-uh." Amy gave up on the search for brownies, took an apple, and went to the sink to wash it. As she did, she peered at her reflection in the microwave window. "How do you think I'd look with bangs?"

"Amy, you're not getting your hair cut."

Amy spun around. "Why not?"

"Because I don't know anything about this contest or this beauty salon."

Amy stared at her mother in disbelief. "Mom! This is crazy! A haircut isn't exactly dangerous, and I'm not going to be kidnapped in a hair salon!"

Her mother's eyes were wide. "Why did you say that?"

"Say what?"

"About being kidnapped. Amy, has someone approached you? A stranger?"

"No, of course not. Who would want to kidnap me? Mom, what's going on? Why are you acting so weird?"

Her mother was beginning to show signs of strain

again. She put a hand to her forehead. "Not now, Amy. I have a headache."

But Amy was too fired up to back down. "Who wants to kidnap me, Mom? My father?"

"Amy, your father is dead!"

"That's what you tell me, but I'm not so sure," Amy shot back. "Maybe that's your secret. Maybe he didn't die. Maybe he's a drug addict or something, and he wants to kidnap me so you'll have to give him lots of ransom money so he can buy more drugs and . . . and, I don't know, something like that."

Nancy looked at her in disbelief. Then she rolled her eyes. "Just one minute, young lady." She went into her office. Amy could hear a drawer opening and papers rustling. Then Nancy emerged with a paper in her hand. Silently she handed it to Amy.

It looked very official. Across the top were the words "Certificate of Death" in fancy, curly letters. Typed in were the name Steven Anderson, a social security number, a date of birth, a date of death, and a place— some country Amy couldn't even pronounce.

"Amy, your father is dead," Amy's mother said again, more gently this time. "Where are you getting these crazy ideas? From Tasha?"

Amy's shoulders slumped. "I don't know. I guess it's puberty."

Nancy stroked her hair. "It's a rough time, I remember. Like you said, everything is changing."

"Everything," Amy said. She allowed Nancy to pull her closer and to continue stroking her hair. "And it's not just that stuff they tell you about in health education. My vision is sharper than anyone else's, my hearing is stronger, I feel so different . . ." Was it her imagination, or had her mother's hand suddenly gone cold?

"Maybe your mother just likes your hair the way it is," Tasha said. It was early Friday evening, and the girls were lying on the floor of Amy's living room, watching music videos. "Mothers can get very tense about things like that. I'm telling you, it's this puberty thing."

"Tasha, my mother is not going through puberty."

"You know what I mean. They don't want us to grow up so fast. Mothers get nervous about their daughters, because we're becoming women. We can have babies and turn them into grandmothers."

Amy rolled her eyes. "I don't think that's what my mother's worried about. You should have seen her face when I asked her if she honestly thought I could be kidnapped at a hair salon. If my father's really dead, who would want to kidnap me?"

For once Tasha was at a loss to provide a possible explanation.

The doorbell rang. "Are you expecting anyone?" Tasha asked.

"No." Amy went to the door. Before she could reach it, her mother came flying down the stairs.

"I'll get that," she said. She peered through the peephole and then opened the door. "Oh, hello, Monica."

"I'm returning your hammer," the neighbor announced. "Sorry I've held on to it for so long."

"That's all right, I haven't missed it," Nancy said. "Come in. What did you do to your hair?"

The girls saw what she was referring to when Monica came into the living room. The red hair was now platinum blond. "Cool!" Amy exclaimed. "You look like Madonna!"

Monica laughed. "I guess that's a compliment. You guys will figure this out sooner or later, but I might as well prepare you. Hair is my hobby."

"Would you like something to drink?" Nancy asked.

"No, thanks, I have to run. I'm going to a gallery opening in Santa Monica. What are you up to this evening?"

Nancy smiled. "Nothing special."

"Why don't you come with me? I have no idea what the exhibit will be like, but there should be some interesting people there."

"Oh, I couldn't," Nancy said. "Thanks for the invitation, but—"

Amy interrupted. "Why not, Mom?"

"Because I don't want to leave you home alone, that's why."

"I could stay at Tasha's tonight. Couldn't I, Tasha?"

"Sure!"

"But I need to fix dinner," Nancy protested.

"We're sending out for pizza tonight," Tasha told her. "Amy can eat with us. There'll be plenty of food."

"And we can grab a bite at a little bistro I know," Monica told Nancy.

"Come on, Mom, go," Amy urged. "You deserve a night out."

Nancy looked torn. "But I can't go like this, and Monica's in a rush."

Monica looked at her watch. "Can you be ready in ten minutes?"

"Sure she can," Amy answered. "Can't you, Mom?"

Nancy bit her lower lip. Then she smiled. "Tasha, go call your mother and make sure it's okay for Amy to stay over. I'll be right back." She ran upstairs, and Tasha went into the kitchen to use the phone.

Amy grinned warmly at the neighbor. "Thanks, Monica."

"Hey, this will be fun for me too," Monica told her. "Nancy and I can figure out who we know in common from school."

"And maybe you can get her to tell you her secrets," Amy said hopefully.

"What kind of secrets?" Monica asked.

"I don't know," Amy said. "Something's bothering her, but she won't tell me anything. If you guys get to be good buddies, she might confide in you. And then you could tell me. But don't tell my mother I asked you to do that, okay?"

Tasha returned. "Don't tell your mother what?"

Unfortunately, at that very moment Nancy Candler was on her way down the stairs. "Amy? Amy, what are you not telling me?"

It amazed Amy how quickly her mind could work under pressure. "I was thinking about dyeing my hair blond."

Relief flooded Nancy's face. "Oh, really?" she said mildly. "You try something like that and you'll be grounded for the rest of your natural life. Did you talk to your mother, Tasha?"

"Yes, and she said we should come home right now because Eric claims he's dying of pizza deprivation. Come on, Amy."

Tasha's house was in its usual state of happy chaos. Tasha's mother was downstairs and her father was upstairs, but as usual they were having a conversation, which meant that they were yelling comments at the top of their lungs. The stereo was blasting. Eric and a couple of buddies were playing a video game and punctuating every move with yelps and shrieks. Amy thought of her own quiet, tense home and hoped an evening out would cheer her mother up.

After pizza Eric took off with his friends, the Morgan parents settled down to watch TV, and Amy and Tasha went upstairs to Tasha's room. "Want to go online?" Tasha asked. "We could check out some chat rooms."

Amy shrugged. "Whatever."

"Or we could make some joke phone calls," Tasha offered. She pulled a phone book off her bookcase. "We haven't done that in ages."

"Don't you think we're getting a little old for that?" Amy asked, but she sat on the floor next to Tasha as she flipped through the phone book.

Tasha giggled. "Remember when we sent two dozen pizzas to Kelly Brankowski when she didn't invite us to her sleepover?"

"I liked when we called that football player from Central High, the one whose picture was in the paper, and I said we met at the beach last summer," Amy remembered.

Tasha nodded enthusiastically. "He really believed you too; he was trying to get you to meet him that night. What was his last name? Jansky, Janoff, something like that."

"Jaleski?" Amy offered. "No, wait, that was the name of the doctor who signed my birth certificate." She began to turn pages rapidly.

"What are you doing?" Tasha asked.

"I'm looking for a J. R. Jaleski, M.D." She ran her finger down a column of names. "Tasha, it's here! Look!"

Tasha leaned over and read the entry Amy was pointing to. "Jaleski, James R., M.D., 1190 Elmwood, 555-2505."

"There aren't any others with the initials *J.R.*," Amy said. "Tasha, this has to be him. This is the doctor who delivered me!"

"Okay," Tasha said. "Now what?"

"I'm going to call him."

"Amy, he probably delivered a billion babies. He's not going to remember anything about you."

"He might. It can't hurt to try. Hand me the phone."

She dialed the number. "It's ringing," she whispered excitedly. There was a click, and then a woman's voice.

"Hello?"

"Uh, could I speak with Dr. Jaleski, please?"

"Who's calling and what is this in regard to?"

This wasn't going to be easy to explain. "He doesn't know me. My name is Amy Candler, and Dr. Jaleski is the doctor who delivered me. At least, he signed my birth certificate, and it says 'attending physician,' so—"

"That's impossible," the woman said sharply. "Dr. Jaleski is not an obstetrician. He's never delivered babies."

"Are you sure?" Amy asked. "It would have been twelve years ago, and the certificate says I was born at Eastside General, only that's not possible because Eastside General wasn't even built then, so it must have been another hospital. Maybe it was an emergency and there weren't any other doctors around, and—"

The woman interrupted again. "What did you say your name is?"

"Amy. Amy Candler."

She could have sworn she heard a sharp intake of breath on the other end. Then there was silence.

"Hello?" Amy asked. "Are you still there? Could I just speak to Dr. Jaleski for a minute?"

"No," the woman replied. "You can't. He's no longer living." Before Amy could react, the line was disconnected.

"What did she say?" Tasha asked.

"It doesn't matter," Amy replied. "Dr. Jaleski is dead."

"Oh. Too bad. You want to try and call that cute football player?"

In the end they played Pictionary and then watched Tasha's beloved video of *Grease,* which they both knew by heart. They sang along with all the songs. Amy didn't think about the woman on the phone until she was in the twin bed next to Tasha's. She went over the brief conversation in her head. Was it her imagination, or had the woman sounded almost frightened? No, there had definitely been something strange in the voice.

Maybe that was why Amy had the dream again. She was in the familiar white place, lying flat on her back and surrounded by glass.

But this time it was as if she was outside her body, looking at herself lying inside the glass. Only she wasn't herself, she was a baby! The baby turned over, so that she was lying on her stomach. And on the upper right side of her back was a crescent moon.

Then the fire started. Amy felt the heat and the fear, and she began shaking. Abruptly she woke up.

For a second panic swept over her as she realized she wasn't in her own bed. Only when she recognized her surroundings did her racing heart go back to a normal pace.

She slipped out of the bed and out of the room to the bathroom across the hall. She closed the door, turned on the light, and stood with her back to the mirror. She pulled down the right strap of her nightgown.

There it was—the crescent moon. It hadn't changed since the last time she'd looked at it. It was no bigger, no smaller. It looked exactly the same. Exactly the same as it looked in the dream. And this meant . . . what?

She went back to bed, half hoping she could return to

the dream when she fell asleep. Maybe she could learn something from it. Maybe it would reveal something to her. . . .

If she did dream anything, she couldn't remember when she woke up the next morning. Over breakfast, she told Tasha about what she did remember.

"So this time, you were a baby," Tasha said thoughtfully. "That's interesting. What did it feel like?"

"I don't know. I'm not even sure if the baby was me."

"But she had your birthmark."

Amy nodded.

"So it must have been you. Hang on a second." Tasha left the table. A moment later she returned with her dream interpretation book and began poring over the index. "Let me see, babies, babies . . . page one-oh-five." She flipped through the pages. "Okay, listen to this. 'Dreaming of one's self as a baby indicates a desire to return to the womb. The dreamer longs for a maternal figure to provide protection and security.' " She looked up. "How does that sound?"

"Are you kidding? My mother's *too* protective." Amy drummed her fingers on the table. "I keep thinking about that woman on the phone last night. Tasha, when I first asked to speak to Dr. Jaleski, she asked me why I wanted to talk to him. Why would she want to know that if he's dead? And then she said Dr. Jaleski is not an obstetrician. *Is* not *was*."

"You think he's alive?" Tasha asked. "But why would that lady lie to you?"

"I don't know. But I want to find out. Tasha . . . let's go there."

"Go where, to his house? By ourselves? Are you crazy?"

"Eleven-ninety Elmwood. Maybe if the woman saw me in person, she wouldn't lie to me. And if I could see her face . . . well, I'd know if she was lying. I'd know if he's really dead."

"Who's really dead?" Eric asked as he ambled into the kitchen.

"None of your business," Tasha replied automatically.

"Where's Mom and Dad?" he asked, pouring cereal into a bowl.

"They went to a wedding, out of town. They won't be back till late."

Eric doused the cereal with milk and joined them at the table. "So who's really dead?"

Before Tasha could give her usual response, Amy spoke up. "J. R. Jaleski, M.D."

"Amy!" Tasha exclaimed. "You're not going to tell him about this, are you?"

Amy nodded. "He could come with us to Elmwood. You said yourself we shouldn't go by ourselves."

Eric looked at Amy in total bewilderment. "What are you talking about?"

Amy told him about trying to find the doctor who had signed her birth certificate. "The woman on the phone was strange, Eric. I don't think she was telling the truth."

"But why would she lie?" Eric asked. "What would be the point?"

"I don't know. Maybe Dr. Jaleski's in some kind of trouble. Maybe she thought I was lying, that I'm not really a twelve-year-old kid. Maybe she thought I wanted to hurt Dr. Jaleski or something."

Eric scratched his head. "You're not making any sense."

"I know," Amy sighed. "But I have to do *something,* Eric. I can't just sit around wondering and worrying. I need to take action. I'm desperate!" She could hear her own voice rising with every word, and that last *desperate* was practically a shriek. Tasha was looking alarmed.

"Amy, it's just a school assignment. You don't want to go crazy over homework."

Amy shook her head. "It's not just homework, Tasha; it's more than that. There's something else . . ."

"What?" Eric asked.

"I don't know! There's a secret, and it's got something to do with my father, maybe, or with my mother, or *me* . . . I *feel* something." She looked at Eric helplessly. He had to think she was losing her mind, or at least letting her imagination go way out of control.

But Eric actually seemed interested. "What does this have to do with finding this doctor what's-his-name?"

"Jaleski, Dr. Jaleski." Amy sighed. "Probably nothing. But I want to check it out."

"Okay," Eric said. "I'll go with you."

"You will?"

Eric shrugged. "I don't have anything better to do."

Tasha found a street map of Los Angeles and spread it out on the kitchen table, and they looked it over. They located Elmwood Road, but it wasn't anywhere near where they lived. Eric, however, had once played a soccer game in a park he recognized on the map. He made some phone calls and determined a bus route.

Amy then called her mother. "Hi, did you have fun last night? Great. Can I go with Tasha to watch Eric play soccer?" She invented a Morgan uncle who would be taking them, assured her mother she'd be home for dinner, and hung up.

Tasha listened and watched in awe. "Wow. Since when did you get to be such a good liar?"

"I'm not sure," Amy said. "I used to be a terrible liar. It's so much easier now, isn't that weird?"

"There's a lot about you that's been weird lately," Tasha commented.

"Yeah, I know." Amy went over to the refrigerator, where a mirror magnet hung. She examined herself. "I don't *look* different. But something's changed . . . I know this sounds crazy, Tasha, but it's like everything's changing. Inside me. I feel different."

Tasha was about to speak, but Amy wouldn't let her. "And if you tell me it's because of puberty, I swear, I'll never speak to you again."

Tasha closed her mouth.

It was a long bus ride, and they had to change buses twice, but there was a tension in the air that kept the trip from being boring. "This is an adventure," Tasha declared happily. "We're on our way to solve a mystery. Do you feel like Nancy Drew?"

Amy nodded. "Who do you want to be? Bess or George?"

Tasha considered this. "Bess was the fat one, wasn't she?"

"Plump," Amy corrected.

"But I don't want to be George. She was the one who looked like a boy. Eric will have to be George."

"How about Ned Nickerson?" Amy suggested, and they both started giggling.

From the seat in front of them, Eric turned. "What are you guys laughing about?"

That only made them laugh harder. Eric frowned. "You kids better get serious. We don't know what we're going to find at this Jaleski house. It could be dangerous."

Amy knew he was just trying to come off as the

macho man who would take charge of the adventure. But she wasn't going to start an argument about that. She was glad he was there with them—not because he was a guy, or because he was two years older. Just because three was better than two if danger was an actual possibility.

Elmwood turned out to be an ordinary street, with small, neat cottages set back from the road. Number 1190 didn't seem unusual in any way.

Amy, Tasha, and Eric approached the front door. Eric raised his hand to the doorbell, but Tasha pushed him aside. "Hey, it's Amy's mystery. Let her ring."

Eric rolled his eyes. "Infants," he growled.

Amy was too nervous to take offense. She pressed the button. The sound of a chime inside the house could be heard. They waited, holding their breaths.

But the chime died away, and no one came to the door. Eric stepped off the porch and went to a window. "The curtains are drawn; I can't see anything," he said.

"There's no car in the driveway," Tasha said.

Amy opened the screen and knocked on the door. She stepped back in surprise as her knocking pushed the door open. Eric jumped back up onto the porch, and the three of them peered into the darkness.

"Hello?" Amy called out tentatively. There was no response.

"See if you can find a light," Tasha whispered.

"You can't break in!" Eric objected.

"We're not breaking in," Amy said, "we're *walking* in." She was thrilled by her own courage as she stepped into the house. With one hand she felt along the wall and located a light switch.

There was nothing remarkable about the room, except for the fact that it was empty.

They moved to the center. "Are you sure this is the right address?" Eric asked.

"Eleven-ninety Elmwood," Amy said. "That was the address in the phone book."

Tasha ran ahead of them and looked in the dining room and kitchen. "There's nothing back here."

Eric went to the little hall off the living room and opened the two doors to smaller rooms. "Empty," he said. "No furniture."

"But I just called this place last night," Amy argued. "And someone was here."

"Well, no one's here now, and it doesn't look like anyone's coming back soon," Eric declared. "Come on, let's get out of here."

Amy just stood there, feeling as empty as the house. She didn't know what she'd expected to find at the address of J. R. Jaleski, M.D., but she thought she'd find *something*.

Eric snapped his fingers. "I know what happened."

"What?" Tasha and Amy asked in unison.

"I have this friend who just moved, and his family kept the same phone number. Only, if you look up his family in the phone book, the old address is listed."

Tasha groaned. "Amy, whoever lived here could have moved months ago. Phone books only come out once a year."

Amy nodded miserably. "Yeah, okay. Let's go." They were heading to the door when Amy remembered they had a long bus ride back home. "Wait a second, I need to use the bathroom."

When she turned on the faucet to rinse her hands, she looked in the mirror and thought her hair was a disaster. She opened her backpack to pull out a hairbrush, but it fell out and settled on the floor under the sink.

She bent down to retrieve it and saw something else. A little brown bottle . . . She picked it up. It was an ordinary bottle of pills; a full bottle, the kind you got at a pharmacy. The label on it gave the name of the pharmacy: Ansonia Chemist. There were an address and phone number for the drugstore. There was also another number with the letters *RX* before it. Amy knew that meant prescription.

And under that number was the name of the person for whom the pills were intended: J. R. Jaleski, M.D.

The name of the medication didn't mean anything to her. But something else on the label did.

She ran out of the bathroom. "Guys, look."

Tasha and Eric examined the bottle. "So what?" Eric said. "That just means he lived here once and forgot some pills when he moved. That could have been ages ago."

"No, look!" Amy pointed to the date in the lower right-hand corner of the label. The prescription had been filled the day before.

nine

What would Nancy Drew do now? Amy wondered. She'd thought they had hit on a real clue the day before when they found that bottle of pills. Not only did it confirm that Dr. Jaleski was alive and had been in the house just the day before, but it also gave them another lead—the pharmacy where the pills had been purchased.

They located Ansonia Chemist without trouble—it was just down the road and around the corner in a small strip mall. And they were in luck—the pharmacy was open.

But that was the end of their good fortune that day. The pharmacist didn't remember filling that particular prescription. The medication was something very ordinary, for an upset stomach. The name Jaleski meant nothing to him. The pharmacist didn't know him.

So what would a real detective do now? Go back to the house on Elmwood and look for more clues? Talk to neighbors, find out if any of them had known Dr. Jaleski or if anyone knew where he'd gone? And was there any point in all this? She might end up finding Dr. Jaleski, only to learn that he remembered nothing at all about her birth. She'd have nothing new for her autobiography.

But of course, now she was thinking that there was more at stake here than her autobiography—

"Amy! Amy Candler!"

The voice cut through her thoughts like a knife. "Yes, Ms. Dealy?"

For once her math teacher was looking at her sternly. "Amy, I have called your name three times. Are you daydreaming?"

"N-Not exactly," Amy stammered.

"Are you aware that there is an equation on the board? The rest of the class has spent the past fifteen minutes working on it. I haven't seen your pencil moving at all. I presume you cannot provide a solution."

Amy looked at the symbols on the blackboard and answered without thinking. "E equals two x minus y."

She knew she had given the right answer, and not

only because of the surprise on Ms. Dealy's face. She just *knew*.

And then she was uncomfortably aware of all her classmates looking at her too. She looked again at the problem on the board. It was a hard one. It was the kind of problem that required at least four steps. She'd always been good in math—but never *that* good.

Ms. Dealy didn't call on her for the rest of the class. But Amy was conscious of knowing the answer to every problem she put on the board—immediately. While all the other kids were scribbling and calculating, all she had to do was scan the figures and the answer was there, imprinted on her brain. It was amazing; it was like magic. It wasn't normal.

Ms. Dealy didn't think so either. She asked Amy to stay after class.

"Amy, if you were any other student, I'd suspect that you saw the answer on another student's paper."

"Ms. Dealy, I wouldn't do that!"

"I realize that. But I also know that you weren't paying attention, and you weren't working on the problem."

Amy had to admit that was true.

"Then how were you able to come up with the answer so quickly?"

Again, Amy was honest. "I don't know."

Ms. Dealy was clearly impressed. Normally Amy

would have felt good about that. But she only felt uneasy.

Something equally strange happened in her next class. She sat down in her seat, prepared for the usual dreary geography experience, and noticed that several of the other students were frantically flipping through the pages of their textbooks. When the teacher came in, they all shoved their texts into the space under their seats and sat up straight, looking at the teacher expectantly. Amy's heart sank. They were having a test today, and in the excitement of the weekend, she'd completely forgotten.

Of course, she'd read the material when it was assigned. But she hadn't gone over it, she certainly hadn't studied it, and Mr. Boring was famous for asking nitpicky questions, the kind that required one-word answers that were either right or wrong. Well, there was nothing she could do about this now, she thought as he handed out the tests. And one bad grade shouldn't pull her average down too much.

She looked at the questions. Peruvian exports, mountain ranges in Uruguay . . . she closed her eyes. And there, in the darkness, she saw the answers. It was as if she'd suddenly developed a photographic memory and each page of the geography textbook was stored in her head. All she had to do was read the question, and she could instantly recall the page that provided the answer. It was bewildering; she didn't understand. All she could do was answer the questions. And she knew that all her answers were correct.

It was like that all day. She couldn't remember ever feeling sharper, quicker, smarter. She knew all the dates of every important event in the American Revolution; she could conjugate French verbs. And it wasn't just her brain that was sharp; she felt physically strong too, stronger than usual. She even climbed a rope all the way to the top in phys ed.

But she didn't feel triumphant and excited, the way she'd felt when she did the triple-back somersault in gymnastics. It was getting a little scary now. More than a little.

She was changing classes and walking down a hall when she saw Ms. Dealy outside the main office. The math teacher beckoned to her, and Amy crossed the hall through the moving stream of students. When Amy reached Ms. Dealy, she realized that the assistant principal was standing there too.

"Mr. Devon, this is the student I was telling you about, Amy Candler. I think we've got a potential state math prize winner here."

Mr. Devon looked at Amy without the slightest sign of recognition in his eyes. He only nodded. But as Amy left them, she heard Mr. Devon murmur, "Excuse me," to Ms. Dealy. When Amy looked up, she found Mr. Devon walking alongside her.

"Ms. Dealy tells me you show an exceptional talent for mathematics," he said.

Amy didn't know quite how to respond without sounding like she was bragging. "I like math," she finally said.

"Are you equally talented in your other academic subjects?" he asked.

Now she had an opportunity to demonstrate that she was no different from other students. "I'm having problems in English."

"Oh?"

"We have an assignment to write an autobiography, and I'm having trouble getting information for it. I don't know much about my background."

"Ah."

He continued walking beside her, but he said no more until they reached her classroom.

"May I offer you some advice regarding the autobiography assignment?"

"Uh, sure."

"Don't worry about your background. Use your imagination. Create your own past."

"But this is supposed to be an autobiography," Amy said. "It has to be the truth."

"Sometimes fiction is more interesting," he said. "And safer." With that, he walked away.

Amy thought that was very strange advice coming from an assistant principal.

Tasha agreed when she met at Amy's locker after class and heard about the encounter. "I think you're right about him. He doesn't act like an assistant principal."

"No kidding." Amy crouched to get a book out of her locker and saw an envelope. "What's this?"

"Someone put a note in your locker?"

"I guess." She opened it. "Oh no, not another one."

"Another what?"

"Oh, I forgot to tell you. I got a nasty note after gymnastics on Wednesday." She handed the new note to Tasha, who read it out loud.

" 'It is imperative that you refrain from demonstrating all your talents in all places, not only in the gymnasium.' What's that supposed to mean?"

"I guess it's because I answered a hard question in math today. That's funny, though. She's not in my math class."

"Who's not in your math class?"

"Jeanine. I'm sure she was the one who wrote me the note after gymnastics."

Tasha nodded. "It sounds like something she'd do."

"But the only class I have with her is English, and we saw a movie today. I don't think I said anything at all."

"Maybe she's got a friend in your math class who told her," Tasha suggested.

"Yeah, maybe." Amy crumpled up the note and tossed it in a wastebasket. Poor Jeanine. She really needed to find better ways to occupy her time.

The director was not pleased with the report he was given.

"I don't like this. She's too curious. She knows about Jaleski."

"She only knows the name. She doesn't know the connection."

The director studied the pages. "Candler. Nancy Candler. Jaleski's assistant?"

"Yes."

"Then there was a conspiracy."

"It would appear so."

The director continued to read. "She asks too many questions."

The man dismissed that. "She's a child."

The director gazed at him steadily. "Do not underestimate her. And keep in mind that she may very well be more than a child." He returned to the report. "What about Jaleski?"

"That's been taken care of."

"She didn't have her hair cut?"

"No."

"What do you propose to do about that?"

"I suggest we proceed with another method," the man said. "She could be taken."

"No," the director said. "If she disappears, her mother will call the police. We don't want to get any official authorities involved and looking into our activities."

"Then what?"

The director told him.

ten 10

Coach Persky was not pleased when Amy told him that her mother wouldn't let her put any more time into gymnastics. "I can't enter you into the regionals without more training," he stated.

"My mother doesn't want me to compete."

"Why not?" he demanded.

That was a tough one. How could she tell him why when she wasn't sure herself?

"She doesn't believe in competition," she offered lamely.

He reacted as if she was speaking a foreign language—there was absolutely no comprehension on his face. "I'll talk to her," he said finally, and started to turn away.

"Coach? Don't bother."

"You don't want me to call your mother?"

"It won't make any difference. She isn't going to change her mind."

His expression was sour, and it was obvious that he was seriously disappointed. "It seems to me that if you were a committed gymnast, you'd show a little more disappointment."

He had to be thinking that if she'd only thrown a tantrum or something, her mother would have given in. And maybe she should have. But she knew that whatever was going on in her mother's head involved something bigger than gymnastics. And suddenly gymnastics weren't that important to Amy either.

Coach Persky could obviously see that. So she wasn't surprised when he paid very little attention to her that day. He didn't even criticize her performance. Of course, she did all her events pretty well—better than well—so there wasn't much to criticize, but she didn't attempt any fancy or extraordinary moves—even though she knew she could do them if she tried.

One person clearly benefited from the situation. Coach Persky devoted more attention than usual to Jeanine. Amy couldn't blame him. After all, Jeanine was the second-best gymnast in the group and the only other person who might have the potential to enter into competition. Still, Amy couldn't help feeling a twinge of jealousy every time Coach adjusted Jeanine's form on the beam, or complimented her landing, or called out encouraging words while she swung from the uneven bars.

Tasha came up behind Amy and whispered in her ear, "You're better than she is."

Privately Amy agreed. Jeanine, of course, was preening under all the attention. Every now and then, she tossed a triumphant smirk in Amy's direction. At least Amy could take some comfort in knowing that Jeanine now had no reason to write her any more nasty notes.

Which was why she was completely surprised when a note did appear, the very next day. It was in the mailbox at home, and Amy was glad Tasha was with her when she found it. It gave her the creeps.

"'It is absolutely essential that you refrain from exhibiting your abilities. You are in danger,'" Amy read aloud.

"Let me see that," Tasha demanded. She read it herself and frowned. "What is her problem? She's Persky's pet now. What else does she want you to do?"

"I don't know!"

"Did you do anything in school today that could have made her jealous?"

Amy thought. "No. Maybe she just wants to make sure I'm not *planning* to do anything." She shivered. "Maybe Jeanine's a lot crazier than we think she is."

"There's something else in your mailbox," Tasha pointed out.

It was an advertising flyer, the kind that appeared all the time in every mailbox in the community. Usually the flyer announced something like a new pizza delivery service or the opening of a dry cleaner's. This one declared the grand opening of Nails Are Us.

"Saturday Only! Free Manicures with This Certificate!"

"Cool!" Tasha exclaimed. "I hope I got one of those."

Amy examined her own nails. "Me too."

"Let's do it," Tasha said.

"I don't know what my mother will say. She'll probably tell me she doesn't want a stranger touching my fingernails."

"Don't tell her," Tasha suggested. "Look at the address! It must be right near the skating rink where Jeanine's having her party. We could go get our manicures first, and then head over to the party with great-looking nails. At least our nails will look good while we're falling all over the ice."

Amy looked at the note she still held in her other hand. "I'm starting to think I shouldn't go to that party. It would be sort of hypocritical, you know? I mean, if Jeanine hates me this much . . ."

But Tasha wouldn't hear of it. "You *have* to go. There's no way I'm going without you. And I want to go."

"Why? You don't know anything about ice-skating."

"Because you know what Jeanine's parties are like. They're fabulous. I heard she's got professional skaters from "Fantasy on Ice" who are going to put on a show. Everyone's going to be talking about this party at school on Monday. And besides, if you don't go, it will give Jeanine a reason to hate you even more. Next time, instead of a nasty note, you might find a bomb in your mailbox."

Tasha had a point. Besides, she'd already bought Jeanine's birthday present. "Yeah, okay, I'll go."

"And we'll get manicures first," Tasha said happily. "Hey, look, there's Monica."

Their neighbor was pulling into her driveway. She honked her horn and waved at the girls. The girls watched her get out of the car with an armful of fabric. They ran over to see what she had.

"I found a vintage clothes store that's going out of business," Monica told them. "Look at all the junk I got!"

Amy gazed at what appeared to be a lot of battered and tattered silk, satin, and velvet. "What are you going to do with it?"

"Fabric art," Monica told them.

"What's fabric art?" Tasha asked.

"I haven't the slightest idea, I just made it up," Monica

said with a grin. "Come on inside and let's see what I've got here."

Inside the house, Monica dumped the colorful pile of material on the living room floor. The girls began to help her sort it by type of fabric.

"Did you have a nice time with my mother Friday night?" Amy asked casually.

"Oh, sure, we had fun," Monica said.

"So what did you guys do?" Tasha asked.

"We went to a gallery and took a look at some really terrible art. Then we had dinner and talked."

Amy couldn't resist. "About what?"

Monica smiled. "She didn't tell me any secrets, Amy, if that's what you're trying to find out."

Amy wasn't surprised. Nancy Candler wasn't the type of person who would open up right away to someone she barely knew. The friendship would have to develop. Besides, even if Nancy had told Monica something personal, Monica wouldn't tell Amy. Adults were like that. They kept each other's secrets.

"Mostly we talked about our days at the university," Monica said. "Even though we didn't really know each other, we had a lot of the same experiences. Oh, and we discovered a funny coincidence. We were both in Washington, D.C., during the same summer, twelve years ago. She was working at a research lab, and I was taking a course in printmaking barely a mile away. And I remember hearing on the TV news about what happened at her lab."

Amy was puzzled. "What happened?"

"It blew up! There was a huge explosion, in August, and it took the fire department all night to put out the blaze. The building was reduced to rubble. Thank goodness it happened at night and no one was there."

"Did your mother ever tell you about that?" Tasha asked Amy.

"No."

"She probably doesn't want to remember," Monica said. "When I mentioned it, I could tell she didn't want to talk about it." She sighed. "I'll never forget that summer. There was a wretched heat wave, and my classroom wasn't air-conditioned. It must have been especially miserable for your mother."

"Why especially?" Amy asked.

"Well, you're twelve, aren't you? So your mother must have been pregnant with you during that summer."

"I was born in August," Amy said. "But I wasn't born in Washington, D.C. I was born right here in Los Angeles. August fifteenth."

Monica's brow furrowed. "Really? That's right around the time of the explosion. I assumed from the way your mother reacted when I mentioned it that she'd been there then."

"Maybe she left right after the explosion," Tasha said,

"and moved here, and had you. Hey, maybe she had you on an airplane! And that's why there's the mix-up on your birth certificate, because she didn't know what state you were flying over when you were born, so she just made up a hospital name after she got here!"

Amy was barely listening to Tasha's fantasy. It wasn't a very satisfactory explanation for yet another mystery about her birth.

When she arrived home, her mother wasn't back from the university. There was a message on the answering machine telling Amy that Nancy had been stuck in a meeting and wouldn't be home till almost seven.

It was only five-thirty now. Amy went into the kitchen in search of a snack. But instead of opening the refrigerator door, she found herself staring at the door of her mother's office.

There weren't any snacks in there. But there could be the answer to a secret.

Naturally her conscience began to whisper: "Your mother is entitled to her privacy. She doesn't want you to go in her office. You have no business thinking about it. Your mother trusts you; that's why there's no lock on her office door."

But for once Amy decided that her conscience was not going to be her guide. She went inside.

She'd been in there before, of course, when her

mother was working at the desk. Nothing looked different now. There were the usual piles of papers to be graded, the computer, the printer, the fax machine, the telephone. But Amy wasn't interested in anything that was clearly visible. Secrets were never left lying on top of a desk.

So she opened drawers. She found pens and pencils, an old lipstick, a bunch of spare change, a receipt for the dry cleaners. In the big file drawer, she found . . . files. She flipped through them, but they all seemed to deal with her mother's courses at the university. One file was labeled Mortgage, another was Car Loan. Nothing looked interesting.

It was after six o'clock now. She moved to the bookshelves and hurriedly surveyed the items. Mostly they were books—big fat biology books. A few books about chemistry and physics. She took a couple of them off the shelf and looked inside, but they were what they appeared to be, and no secrets fell out.

On the top of the shelf were shoe boxes. Amy stood on her mother's chair and opened one of them. It was all tax stuff. The next box contained tax stuff from the year before. She was pretty sure the other boxes would reveal the same.

But she looked in them all, just in case. And in the last box she found something else. A drawing she'd made for Mother's Day when she was six years old.

There were other mementos her mother had saved in there, and they were all about Amy: some old report cards, more drawings, a few photos. And a bracelet.

It was a plastic bracelet, the kind that was put on newborn babies so they wouldn't get mixed up with other babies. Amy wondered why her mother hadn't put it in the baby book with all the other baby stuff.

She looked at it carefully. The letters were faded, but they were still readable. There was the date, her birth date. And her name, Amy. But no last name—that was odd. What was even odder was the fact that her name was followed by a number.

Amy, #7.

e11even

It felt strange to Amy, keeping secrets from her mother.

As an only child and a single parent, they had always been close, closer than most of Amy's friends and their mothers were. They shared everything; they talked all the time. In the evening, over dinner, Amy would report on her day in complete detail. Nancy knew when Amy broke a shoelace; Amy knew when one of Nancy's students got sick over a frog dissection.

Things were different. They both had secrets now.

Amy hadn't mentioned finding the baby bracelet. She couldn't, because then her mother would know she'd been poking around the office. But Amy was going nuts trying to figure out what it could mean. Amy, #7. Was she the seventh baby born in the hospital that day? Or maybe the cribs they put the babies in were numbered. Maybe it was the number of the hospital room where Nancy had stayed.

And why no last name? It could be that her mother hadn't yet decided whether Amy would have the name Candler or her father's name, Anderson. Still, it was strange to see an identification bracelet like that with only a first name and a number.

For the moment, however, she would have to put the mystery out of her mind. She had a more urgent problem to deal with—namely, what to wear to Jeanine's birthday party. The only ice-skating she'd ever seen was on TV, where they wore tutus and spangles. There was nothing like that in her wardrobe.

The closest thing would be a gymnastics leotard. She fumbled through her drawer and found a yellow one. Over that she put on cutoff jeans.

There was a knock on her door. "Amy?"

"Come in, Mom." Amy turned to face her mother as she came in. Nancy looked puzzled when she saw what Amy was wearing.

"You don't have gymnastics today, do you?"

"No, it's Jeanine Bryant's birthday party, remember? You said you'd take me and Tasha. Tasha's mother is going to pick us up after."

Her mother nodded. "But why are you wearing a leotard to a birthday party?"

"It's an ice-skating party. At Hillside Rinks."

"Oh, I see."

Amy turned her back on her mother to take another look at herself in the mirror. Was this particular leotard looking a little grungy? Seeing the reflection of her mother in the mirror, Amy became aware of a strange expression on her face. Nancy was staring at Amy's back.

Uh-oh, Amy thought. Now she's going to want to take me to a skin doctor.

But her mother said nothing about it. "It's going to be cold at the rink, Amy. Put on a sweatshirt."

"But I'll be too warm," Amy protested.

"Then put on a T-shirt, or something," Nancy snapped. "I don't want you running around with a bare back. You'll catch pneumonia."

"Pneumonia! Mom, I've never even had a cold!"

"Just do what I say," her mother said. "And promise me—"

"Promise you what?"

"That you'll keep the shirt on. And you won't take it off, even if you get warm."

"Why?"

"Oh, Amy, can't you just do what I say without asking questions?" her mother cried in a tone of despair.

"Okay, okay, I'll keep my shirt on, I promise." Could her mother possibly get any weirder? Could *anything* get weirder?

In the past few weeks, so much had changed for Amy, changed *inside* her . . . she didn't feel like the same person she'd always been. Sometimes she felt as if she wasn't even occupying the same universe she'd been living in for twelve years.

She'd read lots of books and magazine articles about growing up, about adolescence and puberty, and she knew it was normal for her to feel different, as if she was changing. But this was beyond normal. Nobody could feel the way she was feeling.

When Tasha arrived, she was carrying a book. "What's that for?" Amy asked as Tasha walked into the living room.

"As soon as I take my first fall, I'm going to pretend I twisted my ankle," Tasha informed her. "This is so I have something to do when I'm sitting down for the rest of the party."

Nancy, in the process of dusting the ornaments on the mantel over the fireplace, smiled. "You know, if you were a superstitious person, you'd never say that. You just might twist your ankle for real."

"What's the book?" Amy asked. When Tasha showed her the cover, she nodded. "Oh, yeah, I think I read it.

Isn't that the one about the place where they keep clones to provide spare body parts for other people?"

There was a sudden crash. The little china dog that Nancy had been dusting had slipped out of her hands. It lay in tiny pieces on the floor. Nancy was swaying.

"Mom!" Amy shrieked.

"Mrs. Candler, are you okay?"

They rushed toward her. Nancy put a hand on the mantel and steadied herself. "It's nothing, girls, it's nothing," she said hastily. "That silly accident just startled me. Let me sweep up the pieces and we'll get going."

Fortunately, her mother hadn't paid much attention to Jeanine's birthday-party invitation, which was on the refrigerator door. The card clearly stated that the party began at two o'clock, but Amy told her that she and Tasha had to be at the rink at one. She figured an hour had to be long enough for two manicures.

Only it appeared there would only be one manicure. Tasha was frowning. "I never got one of those flyers," she complained. "I don't understand, everybody gets all the same stuff in their mailbox."

Amy pulled the flyer from her pocket and handed it to Tasha. "You can have mine. I don't care about getting a manicure."

Nancy dropped them off in the parking lot of the

skating rink. They lingered there for a few minutes, to make sure the car was far enough away that Nancy couldn't possibly see them in her rearview mirror. Then they went hunting for the manicure place.

It couldn't have been more conveniently located—it was practically next door to the rink. For a grand opening, the shop certainly wasn't making much of an effort to attract customers. A small card taped to the door identified the place as Nails Are Us. When Amy tried the handle, the door didn't budge.

"I think it's locked," she said.

"Try the buzzer," Tasha suggested.

Amy pressed the button by the door. Barely a second later, it was opened by a tall, sturdy-looking woman with blue-black hair. "Yes?" Then she saw the flyer clutched in Tasha's hand. "Ah, you're here for your complimentary manicure. Welcome! I'm Gloria." She smiled, opened the door wider, and ushered the girls in.

It was a tiny salon. In fact, there was only one place for a customer to sit and have her nails done, and the woman who answered the door appeared to be the only manicurist there. Gloria ignored Amy and devoted herself to Tasha. "Come, dear, have a seat, and look over our color selection." She waved her hand toward a display of tiny bottles and then went to a sink, where she washed her hands as carefully as a surgeon would. Amy, meanwhile, maneuvered herself awkwardly into a corner to watch.

Gloria sat down across the little table from Tasha. "Now, let me see your hands." Tasha obligingly held them out, and Gloria examined them. "These need some trimming," she said, and picked up a small scissors in her hands.

"Aren't you going to use a nail file?" Tasha asked.

The woman didn't answer her. "Have you selected a color?" She carefully clipped the nail of Tasha's pinky finger.

"I can't decide," Tasha said. "Amy, what do you think? Red? Or something wilder, like blue?"

Gloria looked up. Her eyes darted between Tasha and Amy. "Just a minute. Which of you girls received the flyer for the free manicure?"

"I did," Amy said.

"She gave it to me," Tasha added.

Gloria dropped Tasha's hand. "The offer is not transferrable."

Tasha looked at her blankly. "Huh?"

"Only the person who received the flyer can have the free manicure."

"What difference does it make if she gets a manicure or I get a manicure?" Amy asked.

"It's the rule," the woman stated. "I'm sorry, dear."

Uncertainly Tasha started to rise from her chair. Gloria beckoned to Amy. Amy didn't move. "How did you know that it wasn't Tasha who got the flyer?"

The woman stared at her. "Because . . . because the promotion was only sent to people whose first name begins with *A*. Now, take a seat."

"But I don't want a manicure, and she does," Amy protested.

Gloria got up. "Nonsense, dear, everyone wants a manicure." She began to move toward Amy. Amy froze and caught her breath. For some crazy reason, at that moment a manicure was the last thing in the world she wanted.

A buzzing noise cut through the room. Tasha, standing by the door, reached for the handle.

"Don't touch that!" Gloria said sharply, but Tasha had already pulled the door open. A light-haired woman in a business suit stood there.

"What do you want?" Gloria asked her.

The woman flashed something that looked like a badge. "I'm from the state health department. I'd like to see your license."

"My what?"

"The license that certifies you to perform manicures. You have to apply for a license from the health department. Do you have a license?"

"Yes, yes, of course," Gloria said. "I'm not sure where

it is, though. We've just opened, you see, and we're not very organized." She opened a drawer and riffled through it.

"Without a license I have to shut you down," the woman said. "Have you girls been given manicures by this person?"

"She cut one of my nails," Tasha said.

The woman didn't seem concerned. In fact, she wasn't even looking at Tasha. "And you?" she asked Amy. "Did she cut your nails?"

Amy shook her head.

Gloria closed her drawer. "It seems I've misplaced the license."

The woman nodded and turned to the girls. "You can both leave. This place is officially closed."

Outside, the girls looked at each other in bewilderment. "What was that all about?" Tasha asked.

"I don't know," Amy replied. "Maybe the place isn't sanitary or something."

Tasha gazed at her bare nails in mild regret. "I don't care, really. That Gloria gave me the creeps."

Amy nodded. "Me too. I'll bet she's in big trouble now." The girls lingered under the awning of the bookstore next to Nails Are Us to see what would happen next.

"I bet that woman brings her out in handcuffs," Tasha said excitedly. "Maybe she'll be holding a gun on her!"

But that was not the case. The two women emerged. The health department lady spoke to Gloria. "We're watching you. You can relay that to your entire organization."

Gloria had no response. She walked into the parking lot, got into a car, and drove away.

"What did she mean by that?" Amy wondered out loud.

"Gloria's probably got a whole chain of unsanitary manicure shops," Tasha replied. She looked at her hand again. "Ick, do you think I can get a disease from scissors?"

Amy wasn't listening. She was watching as a dark, ordinary-looking car drew up in front of the manicure place. The light-haired woman stepped in on the passenger side, and the car pulled away.

"Tasha, did you see the driver of that car?"

"No, but I'm sure Miss I-Can-See-for-Miles did. Who was it?"

"I'm not sure, but he looked familiar." Amy turned to Tasha. "I know this is going to sound crazy, but he looked like Mr. Devon."

"The assistant principal? What would he be doing with a health department inspector?"

"You got me. Maybe it's his wife."

"And maybe you're just seeing things," Tasha declared. "Your super-vision has gone out of control."

"Yeah, maybe."

They went into the bookstore to kill the forty-five minutes left before the party began. Browsing in the paperbacks, Amy wasn't even aware of what she was looking at. She was thinking, mentally reliving the past few moments. And the more she thought about it, the more certain she became. The woman's voice, the driver of the car—none of it made any sense, but maybe that was because she didn't know *how* to make any sense of it. Each image was like a piece of a puzzle, but she was missing the box the pieces came in. She had no picture to guide her. She had no idea what she was trying to put together.

It was a relief to leave the quiet of the bookstore and go into the skating rink for Jeanine's party. Seeing friends and classmates in a brightly lit setting was a distraction from her disturbing thoughts. The rink was decorated with streamers, banners, and balloons, all pink, Jeanine's favorite color. In the middle of a fancy decorated table stood a huge cake covered in icing with pink and white roses. Great dance music was blasting. It appeared that Jeanine had rented the entire rink for her party.

This was one area in which Amy never tried to compete with Jeanine—parties. Jeanine's parties were major events. This one looked like it wouldn't depart from tradition. On the ice, elaborately costumed professional skaters, feathered and spangled, were spinning and leaping around.

"What color did you get?" Tasha asked Amy when they opened their party favors.

"Pink, of course. What about you?"

"Pink and white stripes."

Linda Riviera, Jeanine's best friend, overheard them. "Did you guys get bangle bracelets?" she asked.

"Yes, Linda," they replied. Linda nodded approvingly. Bangle bracelets were the hot jewelry fashion item of the moment, and Jeanine was sure to give the most preferred item of the year as a party favor.

Amy and Tasha joined the group surrounding Jeanine and presented their gifts to her. Jeanine was all dolled up in a pink spangled skating outfit with matching glitter skates. "Happy birthday," the girls chorused. Jeanine accepted the packages with a big smile and a gushy "Ooh, thank you," as if she was totally surprised that they'd brought gifts. There were no snide smirks today, and she wasn't acting like the kind of person who would write sick notes. It was typical of two-faced Jeanine.

After the presentation of the gifts the girls went to a counter to get their ice skates. A woman behind the booth took their shoes and gave them skates. They sat down on a bench to put them on.

"I wonder if this is like in-line skating," Tasha mused.

"Have you ever tried that?" Amy asked.

"Once. I was okay as long as I didn't try to move."

Amy didn't feel any more confident. Together they

edged onto the ice, clinging to the rail that ran along the edge of the rink. They watched as the professional skaters floated among the crowd, encouraging reluctant, giggling girls to come into the center.

Jeanine, of course, didn't need any encouragement. She was already in the middle of the ice, demonstrating all the jumps and twists she'd learned in her skating lessons. Even Amy had to admit she didn't look half bad. Of course, the fact that none of the other kids were even attempting any real skating moves made her look even better.

Tentatively Amy let go of the rail and was pleasantly surprised to find that she could stand on her own. And she could move. She actually made it all around the rim of the rink without falling.

"How did you do that?" Tasha asked when she returned. She was still struggling along, holding on to the rail.

"It's not that hard," Amy assured her. "Just make like you're walking and let the ice carry you."

Tasha let go of the rail. Her arms flailed wildly, and she would have fallen if Amy hadn't grabbed her. Kelly Brankowski wobbled in their direction and managed to knock them both down. Then another girl crashed into them, and it turned into a chain reaction. They all convulsed in giggles, and the party started to be fun.

They fooled around like that on the ice for a while,

and then it was time for refreshments. After that came the usual cake ceremony, the singing of "Happy Birthday," the opening of the gifts. Amy realized she was actually enjoying herself, probably because it was the first time in a long time that she found herself doing something normal.

Later, back on the ice, the professional skaters put on a performance. The three women and two men demonstrated fancy ice-skating moves, jumps so high they could twist around three times, layback spins, midair splits. One of the men called out, "I'd like to show you some lifts, but I'll need a partner. Where's the birthday girl?"

Giggling and preening, Jeanine skated forward and jumped. The man caught her and lifted her. Then two other male skaters went out into the crowd of girls in search of partners. One of them came very near Tasha, who shrank back in horror. Since Amy was standing right next to her, she found herself being dragged into the center of the rink.

The guy did a little jump, twisting his feet in the air. It looked like fun, so Amy gave it a try. It was surprisingly easy. Then the guy did a layback spin, which looked dizzying, but she tried that too and it didn't make her dizzy at all. The guy was impressed. "Follow my lead," he said. Taking her hand, he began to dance her around the rink.

Amy had never known she could dance at all, let alone on ice. The guy swung her around with so much energy she managed to jump, twirl in the air, and land neatly on one skate with the other leg extended gracefully behind her. The man then tossed her into the air, and she did it again. She became aware of applause, cheers, and cries of "Go, Amy" from her classmates.

She felt fantastic, the same way she'd felt in gymnastics. She could do anything on the ice. She watched one of the women do a triple turn in the air and imitated it perfectly. She began to spin faster and faster, her friends becoming a blur of color racing across her eyes. Then, as she slowed down her spin, she glimpsed their admiring faces—and Jeanine, looking distinctly annoyed. Then Amy saw another face, and she stopped.

He was way over on the other side of the rink, off the ice, and it didn't matter that a camera hid his face. She knew who he was. At the gymnastics center, he had said he was a freelance photographer. Jeanine must have hired him to take pictures of the party. Amy shouldn't be surprised. While other kids would have parents taking pictures at their birthday parties, Jeanine hired a professional photographer. It was a typically Jeanine thing to do.

The party was breaking up. Kids were leaving, but the photographer was still taking pictures. In fact, he seemed to be taking pictures of Amy. She started to skate away in the opposite direction and felt a sudden sharp pain in her ankle. Then she was flat on her stomach, kissing the ice.

She lay there, too stunned to move. All she saw was the pink glitter of Jeanine's ice skates.

She scrambled to her feet. "Jeanine, you tripped me!"

"I did not!" Jeanine declared indignantly.

"And I know why too," Amy continued. "You're jealous."

Jeanine pretended to be incredulous. "Jealous? Of you? Why would I be jealous of you?"

"Because I was skating as well as you without a lesson. Better than you! Because that photographer's taking more pictures of me than you. I guess this means I can expect another nasty note in my mailbox."

Jeanine still looked surprised, only now the expression didn't seem as fake. "What are you talking about?"

"Oh, come on, Jeanine. Didn't you think I could guess who's been writing me those notes?"

"*What* notes?"

Amy hesitated. Something in Jeanine's voice, something about her face, told Amy she was telling the truth. Jeanine looked down. "Yuck, you cut your knee on the ice. It's bleeding." She took a step backward. "Don't let that blood get on my skates."

Amy could see that she needed a Band-Aid. It wasn't exactly a gash, but it was ugly. "Would you like me to ask your photographer to take a picture of it, so you can have something to laugh at?"

"What photographer?"

"The one you hired to take pictures of your party."

Jeanine looked at her blankly. "I didn't hire any pho-tographer."

twelve

Amy's knee was stinging, and a trickle of blood was moving down her leg. She pulled off her T-shirt and tied it around her knee. Trying to ignore the pain, she skated furiously across the ice in the direction of the photographer. Questions crowded her mind. Who *was* this man? Why was she seeing him everywhere? Why was he taking pictures of *her*—and only her? Because that was exactly what he was doing. The camera was pointed in her direction, and he was clicking. By now, she wasn't even surprised that she could hear those clicks from so far away.

"Amy!" Tasha called out. "Over here!"

Amy changed direction and went to the side of the

rink where Tasha was standing. She was surprised to see Eric there too.

"What are you doing here?" she asked him.

"Mom's car broke down, so she sent me to bring you two back on the bus."

"Like we need a bodyguard or something," Tasha added, rolling her eyes in disdain.

The clicking was getting louder. The photographer was right behind her. Amy spun around.

"What are you doing?" she asked him.

"Taking pictures," the man said. "I'm a photographer."

"Yeah, I know," Amy said. "I saw you at the gym. And at my school. And—and in front of my house."

He didn't deny it. "Like I said, I take pictures."

"But why are you taking pictures of *me*?"

Now his eyes shifted back and forth nervously. "Look, little girl, I'm working. I was hired to take pictures here."

"No, you weren't," Amy shot back. "I just asked. No photographer was hired for this party."

The man took a step backward. Then, abruptly, he turned and started walking toward the exit.

"What's going on?" Eric asked in bewilderment.

"That man! He's been following me!"

"Hey, mister!" Eric called after the photographer. "Wait!" The man started running. Eric took off after him.

Amy tried to follow, but she couldn't run in the skates. Frantically she tried to pull them off, but it was impossible—she had to undo the laces first. Finally, with only her socks on, she ran out, with Tasha close behind.

They reached the street and saw Eric coming back toward them. He had a camera in his hand.

"What happened?" Amy asked.

Eric was out of breath, but he was clearly proud of himself. "I tackled him."

"So where is he?" Tasha asked.

"He got away. But I got his camera! We can get the film developed and find out if he's really just taking pictures of you, Amy."

"Okay," Amy said. "I'll go back and get my shoes. And I need to get a Band-Aid too."

"What for?" Tasha asked.

"My knee. I fell and it's bleeding. I can't run around with a T-shirt wrapped around my knee." She untied the T-shirt.

"It's not bleeding. There's nothing there."

Amy looked down and caught her breath. There was no blood on her knee. There wasn't even a mark or a bruise. The cut she'd received no more than ten minutes ago had completely healed. Her head was spinning. This wasn't natural; it wasn't normal!

In a daze, she went back to the ice rink and collected

her shoes, and then she followed Eric and Tasha to a one-hour developer. During the one-hour wait, they went into a fast-food place next door and got sodas.

"What I don't understand," Eric said, "is why a photographer would be after you. You're not a celebrity. And no offense, Amy, but it's not like you're tall enough to be a model."

"Maybe he's a talent scout for an ice-skating show," Tasha proposed. "You were awfully good on the ice, Amy."

"I know," Amy said. "And I've never ice-skated before in my life. How did I know how to skate like that?"

Tasha shrugged. "You could be a natural."

"No one's that natural. All I did was watch those professional skaters, and suddenly I could do what they were doing. Just like in gymnastics—I was doing tricks I'd only seen on TV."

Eric was nodding. "You're a pretty amazing athlete. I remember that basket you made in the driveway. And the way you can run."

"We make jokes about how well I see and hear," Amy went on, "but it's true, I see things and hear things that other people don't. And at school, I read faster, I complete math problems faster . . ." She stopped herself and groaned. "I sound awful, don't I? Really conceited."

"That's okay," Tasha comforted her. "You're still my best friend, even if you are a superior human being."

Somehow Amy managed to look at Eric to see his reaction to her bragging. He didn't appear to be particularly grossed out. "You're different," he said.

"Yes," she said. "I'm definitely different. I'm never sick, I've never even had a cavity. I think I'm more than different. I'm—I'm not normal."

A dead silence followed this statement. Neither of them made any attempt to deny it.

Eric looked at his watch. "The pictures should be ready."

Back at the photo store, they were handed an envelope, which Amy tore open immediately. Eric and Tasha gathered around her while she flipped through them rapidly.

They were all photos of Amy, all taken that week. Amy at school, Amy in gymnastics.

"How did he get back into the gym?" Tasha wondered out loud.

Amy couldn't speak. She was in shock, seeing herself coming out of her house, going into her house. There was even a picture of her sitting in a classroom. "How did he get that?" she asked. "Nobody can get into school who doesn't belong there."

"Maybe he took them from outside, through a window, with a special lens," Eric suggested.

But there was another picture that shook Amy up even more.

"What's that?" Eric asked.

"Your birthmark," Tasha breathed. The crescent moon was distinct and large. "Why would he want a picture of that?"

Amy couldn't answer her. It was another piece of the puzzle—and she had no idea where it fit.

There were no mysterious notes in her mailbox that day when she returned home. But there was an envelope addressed to her, with a return address indicating that it came from an official department of the State of California. She tore it open and read the official-looking, impersonal message quickly.

To Whom It May Concern:
Your request for a copy of the certificate of birth for:

Amy Candler

has been processed.
There is no record of this birth.

The director addressed the group sitting around the table.

"The mission is not proceeding successfully. We have failed to secure hair or nail samples."

"Have you been able to identify the mark on her back with complete certainty?" he was asked.

"No. The photographer claims to have taken a close-range photo, but his camera was stolen."

"Then we still don't know if she is one of them."

"All indications point in that direction. Her appearance. The physical and mental capabilities. The connection between the so-called mother and Jaleski. But we cannot move forward until we have incontrovertible evidence."

Another member of the group spoke. "There is another way to establish this. However, it will require a more complex arrangement."

"Go on," the director said.

"Is there a reliable dentist in the organization?"

thirteen

"I have something for you, Amy," Ms. Weller said when Amy arrived in homeroom Monday morning. "This arrived at school today."

Amy accepted the plain white envelope with her name typed on it from Ms. Weller and took her seat. She didn't open it immediately, though. Envelopes didn't seem to contain good news anymore. What was this note going to tell her—sorry, Ms. Candler, you do not exist?

She took a deep breath and tore it open. It was another official-type letter that looked as if it had been spit out of a computer. In the upper left-hand corner was her name, and under that her student identification number. The message was brief and to the point:

```
Your recent dental examination revealed
a problem that should be treated immedi-
ately in order to avoid more extensive
dental deterioration. An appointment for
treatment has been made for you.
```

This was followed by a date—that day's date—a time, five o'clock, and an address in Sunshine Square.

Amy let out the breath she'd been holding. And she smiled.

"You are most definitely not normal," Tasha said as they dressed for gymnastics that afternoon. "You're not the least bit afraid of the dentist, are you?"

Amy shook her head. "Not a bit," she said cheerfully. She showed Tasha the message she'd received in homeroom.

"Why did this come to school and not to your home?"

Amy shrugged. "I guess because the exam was held at school. And look, the dentist's office is right by the gym, so it's very convenient."

"You're worse than not normal, you're nuts! You act like you're happy about going to the dentist!"

"I know it sounds crazy, but I *am* happy! Tasha, don't you see what this means? I'm not so different after all! I've actually got a cavity or something like that, just like ordinary people. I'm—I'm not perfect!"

Two other girls in the locker room heard those last words and gave each other a look. Tasha and Amy saw the look and choked back a laugh. They had to be thinking that Amy was the most arrogant person on earth.

When Jeanine came in, her eyes went automatically to Amy's bare knee. "Where's your cut?"

"It's all better," Amy said.

"Really? Maybe you shouldn't work too hard in gymnastics today, anyway. I mean, it could still be a little sore."

Amy wasn't going to let Jeanine get on her nerves. "Don't worry about it, Jeanine. I have to go to the dentist." And she sauntered into the gymnasium.

She went directly to Coach Persky. "Coach, I have to leave early today. I have a dental appointment." She spoke importantly and loudly so that others could hear. No one seemed interested, and Coach Persky certainly wasn't impressed. He only grunted.

Before Amy left, she stopped to speak to Tasha. "If I'm not back when my mother comes to get us, just tell her I'll call when I'm through at the dentist, okay?" Tasha agreed, and Amy took off to change and go to the dentist.

The address was a medical office building on the other side of the mall. The message instructed her to report to the office of Dr. Robert Greene, Suite 308. She took the elevator to the third floor and easily located the door. The name Robert Greene, D.D.S. was embossed in gold.

She found herself in a little room with a desk, a small sofa, and an open door that led into a corridor. There was a man on the sofa, reading a magazine, and a woman in white behind the desk. She looked up and smiled at Amy. "Yes? May I help you?"

Amy presented the notice she'd received at school.

"Have a seat," the woman said. "Dr. Greene is with a patient now."

Amy sat down next to the man with the magazine. He ignored her. She saw more magazines lying on a little table, and she got up to take one. She didn't have time to look at it, though. A woman came through the door.

"Will you send the bill to my home?" that woman asked the woman at the desk.

"Yes, of course," the woman at the desk said. Then she turned to Amy. "You may go in now."

Amy looked at the man on the sofa. "I think he was here first."

"I'm early for my appointment," the man said.

Amy went into the corridor. To the right, she saw a

small room with a large reclining chair and all kinds of metal instruments around it. A man in a white coat was standing there. "Amy Candler?"

"Yes."

"Have a seat."

Amy got into the big chair, which was quite comfortable. "What exactly is wrong with my teeth?" she asked.

The dentist's back was to her as he adjusted some instruments on a tray. "Nothing to worry about," he murmured.

"I'm not worried," Amy said. "I'm just curious. What's the problem?"

"Nothing serious," he said. He moved a large piece of machinery so that it was pointing toward her.

"What does that do?"

"It takes X rays of your teeth. It won't hurt; don't be afraid."

"I'm not afraid."

Now he was bending over, fiddling around with something on the floor that looked like a tank, and she could hear a hissing sound. "What's that?"

"Nitrous oxide. It will help you relax."

"I'm already relaxed," she assured him. In her opinion, he was the one who seemed nervous.

"Well, this will keep you from feeling any pain."

"You just said it wouldn't hurt."

He was holding a contraption in his hand, and he started to put it on her face. Automatically she turned away.

"Haven't you ever been to a dentist before?" he asked.

"No."

"This is a perfectly normal procedure."

Well, if it was the normal thing to do . . . She let him place the mask on her face.

"Now breathe in deeply," he instructed. "I'll be back shortly."

Actually it was okay, breathing through the mask. The air didn't smell bad at all; in fact it was sweet. She didn't feel particularly drowsy, just calm and peaceful. She looked up at the ceiling. It was blue, a deep greenish blue, like the Pacific Ocean on a clear day . . . There were no waves, of course.

This really was a very comfortable chair. How nice she felt . . . Images of herself wandered through her head. Ice-skating, sailing over the ice. Gymnastics, the uneven bars, flying through the air. If she concentrated, she could almost hear the music in her memory of the ice-skating rink. She could also hear a voice, coming from outside the room.

Words drifted to her ears . . . "We don't know how she'll respond to the radiation from the X rays. It's impossible to make predictions at this stage. . . ."

Predictions . . . Tasha had once visited a gypsy fortune-teller at a fair who made predictions. Only she couldn't remember them after . . .

"I understand how important she is, but you have to remember, we're dealing with a completely unique genetic makeup here."

Makeup . . . when would her mother let her start using eye shadow? There were so many pretty colors . . .

". . . she may require a higher dosage than is usually given . . . there's the potential for chromosomal damage . . ."

Amy stirred restlessly in the chair. She didn't like these words; they were bothering her. She'd rather concentrate on flying over a rainbow . . .

"If you're right about her, she's a mutation, there are no guidelines . . . How old is she? Twelve?"

How strange, he was talking about her. A mutation . . . did that have anything to do with puberty? The rainbow was gone; she didn't feel like flying now. Of course it wasn't a real rainbow; this gas was making her see things. And was she really hearing these words, or was the gas making her think she heard them?

"Look, I said I'll be careful, but I can't promise you she'll come out of this in the same condition. We're not dealing with a normal human being here!"

That word, her favorite word, *normal* . . . it cut into

the hazy fog that filled her head, like a red light, a warning, flashing—danger, danger, danger. With effort, she raised a hand and brought it to her face.

The dentist returned. "Don't touch that mask!" he said sharply.

She tried to talk, but her lips were moving in slow motion. "Whuhht . . . arrr . . ." Now he had his hand on her chin and was pulling her mouth open wider. He was putting something inside, something that felt like card-board, but something was wrong. Why wouldn't her body obey the orders her mind was screaming . . . Get out, get out, danger, danger? With all the energy she could gather, she bit down.

The dentist shrieked and pulled his hand back. Somehow, at that moment, her hands responded to the signals from her brain, and she managed to rip the mask off. Still grimacing in pain, the dentist grabbed her wrist with his good hand and tried to press the mask back down on her face. But she'd had a breath of real air now, and she could feel her strength and her consciousness returning. She pushed back on his hand, and for a moment it was as if they were arm-wrestling. She leaped off the chair, still pushing his hand back. And then she had the mask on *his* face. He fell back, onto the floor. She fell on top of him, and they struggled as he tried to get the mask off.

"Amy! Amy!"

"In here!" she screamed.

The door was kicked open, and there stood Coach Persky. Behind him, her face white, was her mother, and by her mother's side was Tasha.

The dentist was struggling to his feet, and the coach lunged at him. The dentist flung out an arm, practically knocking Tasha down, but Coach moved to support Tasha, and the dentist fled. Coach Persky ran after him while Nancy sank to the floor and took Amy in her arms.

"Oh, my baby, my baby," she crooned, rocking Amy back and forth as if she really was a baby. And Amy had the strangest vision . . . for a very brief moment, she was back in her dream, the recurring dream, with the fire all around, but she was out of the glass and in her mother's arms.

"Mom? Mom, what's going on? Tell me," she begged.

But her mother just kept holding her and rocking her.

Coach Persky returned. "He got away with the others," he growled. "Is she all right?"

Nancy seemed to have recovered some composure. "Yes, yes, she's fine." She rose, and Amy rose with her.

On the way out of the building, Coach Persky told Amy how her mother had arrived at the gym to pick her and Tasha up; how upset she'd become when she learned that Amy had gone to see a dentist; how she'd insisted that Amy was in danger—and how fortunate it was that Tasha had seen the message telling Amy where the dentist's office was.

"What I don't understand," Tasha said to Amy's mother, "is how you knew Amy was in trouble. Going to the dentist is pretty gruesome, but it's not usually dangerous."

Nancy just shook her head.

"Mom? How *did* you know?"

"A mother's intuition," Nancy murmured.

But Amy knew that couldn't possibly be true. And the expression on her mother's face, the combination of awe and despair, only confirmed this.

fourteen 14

"**B**ut why do we have to move?" Amy trailed after her mother into the bathroom.

"I can't explain now, Amy. Trust me, we have to do this." Nancy opened a cupboard and pulled out a stack of towels. Amy followed her back into the hallway, where she dumped them in a box.

"Where are we going?"

"Amy, please, no more questions. I'll explain later. Go—do something. Watch TV, anything."

"I'm going to call Tasha."

"No! Don't call anyone, Amy. No one can know what we're doing. Not even Tasha."

"Not even me?"

Nancy's voice softened, but the anxiety was still there. "Later, Amy. When you're safe."

Safe, Amy repeated silently. Safe from what? Homicidal dentists?

The evening before, when they'd returned from the ordeal, her mother had sent her to bed. Then Nancy had gone into her office, where she'd spent hours on the phone. Amy could hear her tapping at the number pad as she dialed, but her mother's voice was so low that Amy couldn't pick up on what she was saying, not even with her supersharp hearing.

Today she'd told Amy she wasn't going to school. Then the boxes had been delivered. And the morning had been taken up with packing.

"Mom?"

"*What?*"

"How come I'm not safe here? What's the danger? What was that dentist trying to do to me? Tell me!"

Her mother finally faced her. "I can't tell you anything else, Amy. It's for your own protection. And I'm begging you, please stop trying to know. It won't do you any good; it can only hurt you." She took Amy's hand and gazed intently into her eyes. "Do you love me, Amy?"

"Of course I love you, Mom!"

"Then do one thing for me. Don't ask me any more questions."

"Ever?"

"Just . . . not now."

"One question," Amy pleaded. "And if you answer this one, I promise, I'll never ask another. Mom . . . I'm not normal, am I?"

Love and sadness flooded her mother's face. "You are absolutely perfect."

Amy's heart sank.

She went downstairs, the words reverberating in her ears. "You are absolutely perfect." If Tasha had been there, she'd have told Amy that all mothers said that to their daughters. But Amy was sure they didn't say it the way her mother had said it. As if it was true.

And then Amy understood why her mother had reacted the way she did the day before, rushed to the dentist's office, knew that Amy shouldn't be seeing a dentist. Because there was no reason for her to see a dentist, or a doctor, ever. Because she couldn't have ailments or injuries like other people. The cut on her knee, the one that had healed in minutes . . . that wasn't normal. Amy wasn't normal.

What *did* that dentist want from her? It had something to do with X rays, she remembered that. Dental X rays . . . and then she thought about the manicure she was supposed to get. And the haircut she had won. Teeth, fingernails, hair . . . she drew her breath in. For the first time, a few of the puzzle pieces were linked. She'd watched enough detective shows to know that teeth, fingernails, and hair could lead to an identification.

But why would anyone want to identify her? Why was she perfect? Why was she in danger? So many questions, and no one to ask.

She wandered into the kitchen. Through the open door, she could see the contents of her mother's office, crammed into boxes. One folder remained on the desk, next to her mother's briefcase. Amy went into the office and opened it.

Major disappointment. It was her mother's personnel records, from the university. There were her résumé, school transcripts, letters of reference. Very uninteresting stuff. After that came the medical report from Nancy's last physical. As far as Amy could tell, her mother was in perfect health. All she learned was that her mother had had her tonsils out when she was six years old. After that, everything was checked No: no heart problems, no mental problems, no history of chronic disease, no evidence of pregnancy or childbirth . . .

No evidence of pregnancy or childbirth.

Nancy Candler had never been pregnant. Nancy Candler had never given birth. Nancy Candler wasn't anyone's mother.

"Amy! What are you doing in my office?"

Amy made no effort to defend herself. She turned slowly to face her mother—no, not her mother. Whoever she was. Silently she pointed to the item on the medical form.

Emotions rushed across Nancy's face. Shock, anger, horror, sadness . . . and then, finally, resignation.

"Not later," Amy said. "Now."

Nancy nodded. She sat down at the kitchen table. Amy sat down across from her.

Nancy spoke in a monotone, with a slight tremor in her voice and a hint of tears.

"I don't know where to begin."

Amy did. "I wasn't born at Eastside General Hospital. I wasn't born in California."

Nancy nodded. "Almost thirteen years ago, I was living in Washington, D.C., working in a government research facility. I was involved in a highly confidential project. Noted scientists of all types had been gathered—medical doctors, geneticists, physicists. I was the assistant to an eminent biologist, Dr. James Jaleski."

Amy's eyebrows went up at that name, but her mother didn't notice. And Amy didn't want to interrupt.

"The project was code-named Crescent. I don't know why, it was just a word. But the mission was monumental. We were directed to collect chromosomes and other genetic material from humans of exceptional form—people with superior health, intelligence, talent. We were told that our investigations, our pioneering efforts, could result in the identification of a means by which to extend human life, eradicate disease, eliminate birth defects, develop the means to correct the mistakes of nature. We thought we were working for the benefit of all humanity. We believed we were doing something pure and noble and good."

Amy had to break in. "I don't understand. What did you do with this genetic stuff?"

Nancy bowed her head. "We created life, or the basis of life. We cultivated embryos in a laboratory, under controlled conditions and constant observation. Thirteen identical female life-forms, derived from a combination of superior genetic material. They were called . . . Amys."

"You made . . . babies?"

Nancy almost smiled. "We didn't call them babies. We needed to distance ourselves. So we called them organisms, entities, subjects . . ."

"Clones?"

"Yes. Clones."

Amy felt strangely calm. It was almost as if she'd known all along. She pinched her own arm, and it hurt. She still felt like a real person. "What happened?"

"One of the project members made a horrifying discovery. Our work was not intended to benefit humankind. A small but powerful group hidden within the national government bureaucracy had employed us to create an elite human species, a superior type of people. A master race."

"Why?"

"We never knew. Probably for some kind of world control. All we knew was that their motives couldn't be good. And we knew we had no alternative but to destroy the project."

"The babies," Amy corrected her.

"We thought that as cold, impersonal scientists, we could do this. The notion of allowing a master race to develop was so appalling, you see, and this would be the lesser of evils. But we had a conscience, we had ethics, we had feelings. So while we were able to eliminate all evidence of our work that existed on paper, or in computer memory, we could not destroy the most significant product. We could not kill the Amys."

How odd to think of herself in the plural. But then Amy recalled her dream. She wasn't the only one in a glass cage. There were other glass cages.

"A fire," Amy said.

"Yes. We had set a device to explode at a specific time.

But something went wrong, and the spark ignited early. The Amys had been evacuated—all but one. Number seven."

"Me."

Nancy nodded slightly. "The other scientists told me it was too late, that the entire laboratory would explode in minutes, maybe seconds. But I ran back inside and took you out of your incubator."

"I remember," Amy said, too softly for Nancy to hear.

"We had planned to send the Amys all over the world for adoption, far enough apart so that they could never find each other. I had no intention of keeping a—a baby. But when I ran from that burning laboratory, with you in my arms, and I looked into your eyes—well, you can see what happened."

Amy nodded. She was absorbing all this without too much difficulty. It was unbelievable. Yet it made perfect sense.

"Who is Steve Anderson?" she asked.

"A guy I knew at UCLA. We dated a few times, though it was never a serious relationship. He was nice. And after I moved back here with you, I learned from the alumni magazine that he'd been killed in an accident. I sent for a copy of his death certificate. I had the magazine photo enlarged and put it in a frame. Through . . . through professional connections, I was able to obtain forgeries of a birth certificate and everything else you'd need to enter school. I invented a history to tell you when you were old enough to ask questions. I guess it wasn't very convincing." She smiled sadly. "I never had much of a creative imagination."

"But didn't you think I'd ever realize how different I am?" Amy asked her.

"No, because at first, you weren't different at all! You were a bright baby, healthy, beautiful, but normal! I assumed that our experiments in creating a superior life-form had failed. Which was fine with me, because I had a lovely little girl. I could never take you to a doctor, because any blood tests might reveal your unusual genetic composition. But that was okay, because you were never sick."

"But now . . . ," Amy murmured, and Nancy continued.

"Yes. Now, my little girl started to become a woman. And the effects of the experiment began to appear."

So Tasha was right, Amy thought. Everything *can* be blamed on puberty.

But this still didn't explain it all. "Why are we leaving?"

Nancy took a deep breath. "Because they know you exist."

"They?"

"The group that initiated the project. We assumed they believed us when we reported that all the Amys had died in the fire. But that dentist yesterday—I believe he is one of them. They want to find you. They thought they could identify you through your teeth."

It was all coming together. "They haven't given up," Amy said. "They still want to create a master race."

"Yes," Nancy said. "And they believe they can. Through you."

The puzzle pieces were assembling in Amy's head. She knew now why she'd won a haircut in a contest she'd never entered, why she'd received an offer for a free manicure when Tasha hadn't. She understood why her mother didn't want her to get into gymnastics competitions. Fame was not something she should aspire to.

Still, there were so many questions, questions about Dr. Jaleski, about Mr. Devon at school—and about the other Amys. Where were they now? And had *perfect* boys been created in some other laboratory?

"Mom," she began, and then realized how easily the word had slipped out. Because it still felt natural, despite everything.

The phone rang. Her mother stared at it for a few seconds, the fear evident on her face. Then she picked it up. "Yes?"

She said nothing else. And strain as she might, Amy could only pick up bits and pieces of the voice on the other end of the line: "No escape . . . cannot hide . . . influence . . . power . . ." And one complete sentence:

"She will have to learn to protect herself." Amy thought she recognized the voice. It was the voice that had told her to invent her autobiography.

Finally Nancy hung up the phone. Then she reached out and stroked Amy's head.

"We're staying, aren't we?" Amy asked.

"Yes."

f i f t e e n 15

"**Y**ou're awfully quiet today," Tasha said as they walked to school the next morning. "Are you still freaked out about what happened at the dentist?"

"Yeah, I guess so," Amy said.

Eric's eyes were bright with admiration. "Tasha told me how you tackled him. That's cool. I wish I could have seen that!"

"I wonder if they'll ever catch him," Tasha said.

"Yeah, and I want to know why he was after you," Eric chimed in. "Maybe he thought you were somebody else. Like the daughter of a movie star, and he could hold you hostage for a huge ransom."

"Yeah, maybe," Amy said.

They separated inside the school building. Amy didn't go directly to her homeroom. She stopped by the assistant principal's office first. The door was open, but no one was inside. The secretary appeared behind her. "Yes? What do you want?"

"I was looking for Mr. Devon."

"Mr. Devon is no longer with us," the secretary told her.

"What?"

"Mr. Devon left this position yesterday." The secretary looked distinctly annoyed. "He quit, with no notice, just like that!" And she snapped her fingers.

"Where did he go?" Amy asked.

"I have no idea," the secretary replied. "You'll have to speak to the principal."

Amy didn't bother.

All morning she moved through her classes as if nothing had changed. To her classmates, to her teachers, she was Amy Candler, no different, nothing special. That was how it would have to be. Her mother had made that very clear to her. And now Amy understood why.

Later, in English class, the students gave the oral presentations of their autobiographies, a summary of what they had written. Amy was the fifth to stand before her class. "I was born in Los Angeles," she said. "My father died before I was born, in an accident. My mother teaches biology at a university." She went on to describe her interests and hobbies, her favorite foods and movies and TV shows, and all the other ordinary stuff every other student had told the class. At the end of her oral report, she said, "It's clear that my life has not been filled with adventure and excitement. In fact, it's a very quiet life. I'm just an ordinary twelve-year-old girl, and there's nothing remarkable about me."

There was the usual scattering of applause from her bored classmates, and a triumphant smirk from Jeanine, whose autobiography had made her sound much more interesting.

It was hard for Amy to take that from her rival. But that was what she had to do.

For now.

The director addressed the organization.

"We knew this would not be easy," he said. "And it has become more difficult than we could have ever anticipated."

He was asked, "Is there any point in expending more effort in this direction?"

The director fixed cold eyes on the speaker. "We are talking about the future of natural history, the development of civilization. Yes, I believe there is a need to expend more effort."

Another member spoke. "If we terminate this direction now, we could devote our energies to exploring alternative means of achieving our goals. There could be others out there. They would serve our purpose just as well."

The director shook his head. "There is a saying: 'A bird in the hand is worth two in the bush.' "

"You recommend that we should continue our focus on this subject?" he was asked.

The director nodded. "We have only just begun."

Don't miss

replica

#2

Pursuing Amy

It was a nice night out. The rain had stopped, and there was a pleasant breeze.

Amy and Eric walked in comfortable silence. Then Amy stopped.

"What?" Eric asked.

"Do you hear something?" she asked.

"No."

It was easy to forget how superior her hearing was to other people's. "I guess it's just the wind," she said. But after another few steps, she stopped again. Her pulse quickened. "No, it's not the wind. It's something else."

"Like what?"

Amy swallowed hard. "Footsteps. When we stop, the footsteps stop. But they're getting closer."

"You've been watching too many horror movies," Eric told her.

Was she letting her imagination run away with her? She concentrated on the sound.

No. They were real footsteps. Very real. And they were getting louder. Someone was following them. "Eric, we have to walk faster."

Eric still looked doubtful, but the urgency in her voice must have gotten through to him. He picked up his pace. As they walked, she listened. The footsteps behind them were quickening too.

She tightened her grip on Eric's hand. "Why would anyone follow us?" Eric asked in bewilderment. But by now he could hear the steps. His grip tightened. "Maybe we should knock on someone's door. Or flag down a car."

But there was no time for that. The tempo of the footsteps behind them had increased.

"Eric, run!"

Amy took off, moving so fast the trees and houses went by in a blur. She had no idea how far she'd gone until she heard her name being called from way behind her. Suddenly she realized she no longer had Eric's hand and that the voice was his. She stopped and whirled around. The street was dark, and there were no street-lamps. But she could see Eric. He wasn't alone.

Without thinking twice, and with every ounce of strength she could muster, Amy tore back in his direc-tion. As she got closer, she saw a man struggling with Eric. Eric was doing his best to defend himself, but the man was too powerful. Then, as soon as he spotted Amy sprinting back, the man let go of Eric's arm. She knew he was preparing to take her on.

Amy didn't try to sidestep the man. She lowered her head and barreled right into him, knocking him to the ground. He appeared to be stunned but not knocked out, and Amy wasn't going to give him time to recover and get back on his feet. She reached out for Eric's hand and they took off running. This time she controlled her pace so he could keep up with her. Any minute now the man would catch up to them. She kept her eyes peeled for a hideout. When she made out the form of a play-house behind a cottage, she tugged hard at Eric's hand so he would turn with her.

They made it off the main road just in time. She could hear the man running and panting behind them. He couldn't have seen them leave the road.

The playhouse door was open. They got down on their hands and knees and crawled inside. "Amy—"

"Shhh!" They crouched under the low roof. She could hear the footsteps drawing closer. Then she heard some-thing else—a car. It screeched to a halt.

"She's not up this way," a voice declared.

"She must have cut through the alley."

A car door opened and shut. When the sound of the motor faded away, Amy let her breath out.

She looked at Eric. Even in the pitch-black darkness, she could see that his face was pale. "Are you okay?" she asked.

His voice was thin. "Yeah. Are you?"

"I'm okay. I think they're gone. But we'd better stay here for a few minutes."

"Amy, what's going on?"

Her mind raced as she tried to come up with an answer. What could she blame this on? Muggers? Kid-nappers? Drug addicts? Generally crazy people roaming the streets of L.A.?

"That guy," Eric said. "He caught me, but he let me go. He only wanted you. Why?"

Nothing came to her, nothing that would sound even halfway believable. Except the truth.

"Eric . . . I want to tell you something."